Evildoing at Easter in Edgemont

Village of Edgemont, Volume 4

Della North

Published by Lynda French, 2025.

EVILDOING AT EASTER IN EDGEMONT

First edition. May 27, 2025.

Copyright © 2025 Della North.

ISBN: 978-1998074501

Written by Della North.

Table of Contents

To Nessa Mackenzie, my greatest fan, with sincere thanks for your encouragement and with love to you.

Front Matter

About "Evildoing at Easter in Edgemont"

The insidious reach of organized crime penetrates Edgemont when a stripper is found dead on the steps at Edgemont School for Girls. But the case, an apparent drug overdose, isn't as cut-and-dried as it first appears and when the evildoing is revealed it opens up a long list of suspects.

With George Grant busy following leads Judith Taylor is left to fight her first battle of Principal versus the School Board on her own with support from Pat Johnson.

Lila Morelli is pregnant and struggling with her emotions, Brian Penner is confused, and Judith is overwhelmed by wedding arrangements. Everyone is trying to cope with the big changes they're facing.

This fourth novel in the Village of Edgemont Cozy Mysteries series sees the return of familiar characters, their relationships continuing to develop, while a crime is solved.

About the "Village of Edgemont" series:

Judith Taylor, bursar at Edgemont School for Girls, is reluctantly dragged into murder investigations but with the help of the school nurse, also her best friend, Lila Morelli; and the handsome policeman, a different kind of close friend, Detective George Grant; Judith strives hard to find justice.

Old friends and new characters appear throughout the series, and romance is always in the air.

The fictional small town of Edgemont is located in the foothills of the scenic Rocky Mountains in Alberta, Canada

"Really, really enjoyed the story and found it difficult to put down, the tension built up so well."

"Fabulous twist in this one."

"Twists & turns, action and drama fill the pages of these books. Fun reads!

"This Christmas story moves the characters through 2020 and into the new year. I really enjoy how their romances evolve, and especially like the choice Reg makes."

The Main Characters of the Series:

Judith Taylor was a reserved woman in her early thirties living a solitary life with no family or friends until she unwillingly became involved in a police investigation led by Detective George Grant. Judith worked as the Bursar at the Edgemont School for Girls for several years but when Principal Patricia Johnson retires she recommends Judith as her replacement.

George Grant, known as "Grant", fought his attraction towards Judith until a threat against her life pushed the two of them closer together. Although commitment-shy he is forced to recognize the depth of his feeling for Judith when another man takes an interest. He has finally proposed and they need to set a wedding date.

Lila Morelli, the Nurse at the Edgemont School for Girls, has steamrollered Judith into forming a friendship using her vibrant personality. Lila's marriage has ended and she's now pregnant and engaged to Brian Penner.

Brian Penner, a widower, is a General Contractor with his own construction company. He met Lila when his daughter Beth went missing and her kindness drew him in. He quickly commit to a serious relationship and their baby is due at the end of July.

Beth Penner, Brian's daughter, a student at Edgemont School for Girls, who has boyfriends.

The Crime

Good Friday 2021

Gayle Boudreau overdosed on a deadly drug in the early hours of April 3rd, long after the government-mandated 11:00 pm closing at the club where she worked. Spring had arrived less than two weeks prior and the damp air made for a chilly pre-dawn.

Although take-home kits of *Naloxone*, the short-term solution for opioid poisoning, are available for free province-wide, the medicine can't be self-administered and Gayle was alone. At least that's what the police first thought, back when they believed hers was a death by misadventure.

Her day was a mix of chaos and conflict, the kind of haywire atmosphere Gayle actively generates, feeding off the static-electric vibes.

She woke, far too early in her opinion, in a foul temper. She'd just spent her third uncomfortable night on the living-room couch at her mother's place in the Edgemont Trailer Park.

Having absconded with the rent money from her boyfriend, ex-boyfriend now, Gayle had no where else to go.

Cherysh Boudreau wasn't welcoming. The rough-and-tough woman has a full-time day job plus works part-time a couple of nights a week so she has no sympathy for spongers. She made it clear Gayle will have to contribute her share.

The household consists of Cherysh's 17-year-old son Harry, her 13-year-old daughter Didi, and current boyfriend Norm who only moved in recently. Norm works shifts so the couple can't spend a lot of time together but given Cherysh's volatile temper that's probably good for their relationship.

With four residents and a temporary guest the mobile home, even though it's a three-bedroom double-wide, is feeling cramped. They all share the one full-size bathroom and Cherysh has an *en suite* toilet and shower that she doesn't share.

Until now Gayle has managed to dodge her mother's demands with promises of a payment coming soon but it's the long weekend. Holidays both today, Good Friday, and on Easter Monday, mean her siblings will be off school and her mother isn't working either. She's currently out with Norm, but Gayle won't be able to avoid her much longer.

Gayle figures her take-home from tonight and tomorrow night stripping at the club will be enough to pay what her mother wants. She just has to get through the next couple of days. Unfortunately, as Gayle half-jokingly admits herself, *money doesn't burn a hole in her pocket, it only warms the lining*. She spends it as fast as she gets it.

She's a light-fingered girl who steals anything anyone leaves lying around. At work that's usually just make-up, disposable lighters, and costume jewelry not the cold, hard cash she needs. Since moving into the trailer she's already discovered and stolen the bit of money her little sister had stashed away.

Right now her dilemma is what to do with the brick of cocaine she found hidden away at the club. Gayle took it with only the vaguest idea of how to sell it.

Snorting a laugh to herself Gayle knows her mother sure won't accept it in lieu of rent money. *In fact*, Gayle thinks, *if Cherysh finds out she'll freak just over having drugs in her home*. Over the years Gayle has watched her mother become a hard, intolerant woman.

Continuing her havoc-wreaking Gayle borrows her brother's car without asking. *I don't know how long he's gonna be gone*, she rationalizes, not willing to wait. Gayle literally twists her sister's arm to make Didi reveal where Harry hides his keys. *You can't take Harry's car, they took away your driving licence*, cries Didi, but Gayle ignores the girl.

Gayle is a poor driver, though. *En route* to her other boyfriend's workplace she clips a garbage can and runs over a curb, complaining the whole way about having to drive such a crappy car.

Waltzing into the parts shop she drops the bombshell that she's pregnant and what will he pay to keep that quiet from his wife? Clay calls her a lying bitch and slaps her face but Gayle just grins at him knowing she has the upper hand.

She's enjoying herself, thrilled at besting him, needling and provoking him. It's not the way a man looks that attracts her, but the way he looks at her. A sardonic smirk that says *I know all I need to know about you, darlin'*. It doesn't matter if his eyes are a cool blue or a warm brown so long as they size her up and look right through her. It's the challenge to be seen that drives her.

Clay is seeing her now as they argue back and forth, but this time he isn't going to roughly grab and kiss her. Instead, he caves in and promises to get some money together. She should be elated but her confidence is faked when she sashays out with a warning *that you better!*

He continues cursing Gayle in her absence until he looks up and catches the sidelong glances of a couple of employees. Snarling that *the show's over* he stomps to the front door and stands with his arms folded tightly across his chest.

Adding a little extra wiggle to her walk in case Clay is watching, but half-hoping he isn't so he won't see the old beater she's driving, Gayle smirks to herself before sliding behind the wheel. Clay is already on a final warning from his wife so he'll be damn sure to co-operate.

Gayle really is pregnant and figures the odds are pretty good that the baby is Clay's but she's not worried about proving it. Obviously if she was going to keep it he'd insist on a paternity test before shelling out eighteen year's worth of child support, but abortions are free and he'll pay her off to ensure she gets it done right away.

She'll tell him she needs a few weeks off work to recover so he'll have to cover her earnings, too.

Driving away she laughs out loud, revelling in the power she holds over the man. It's a good thing she didn't look back or the murderous look on his face would frighten her.

Blissfully unaware she heads back to the Edgemont Trailer Park and is nearly home when the damn car suddenly slows right down. She manages to steer it onto the shoulder of the road before it dies. Fuming over *this piece of shit car* Gayle gets out and finishes her trip on foot.

Arriving home later than she'd planned her mood is poisonous when Harry confronts her in a fury. Gayle pushes her brother aside with a hard shove to his chest and heads straight to the bathroom. The noise of the shower makes it easy to ignore his yelling.

Finished, she wraps herself in a towel before coming out to holler right back at him that his stupid car broke down and is stuck on the side of the road.

"What? Where? Where's the hell is my car? Jeez Gayle, you are... you're just... you're such a–" the teenager chokes on his words, struggling to hold back angry tears.

Didi grabs her brother by the arm to drag him out of the trailer saying: "C'mon, Harry let's go find your car before anybody does anything to it. It's a holiday and lots of guys are just hanging around and, well... you never know."

The two young people leave and Gayle starts putting together her outfit for work. Normally she'd get ready at the club but she's on the outs with the other dancers and knows she might get slapped around in the dressing-room. No point putting herself at risk of a hair-pulling, kicking and screaming cat-fight.

Since she's alone Gayle isn't bothered when the towel drops off. She searches through her suitcase on the hide-a-bed trying to pair up a matching set of lingerie when the trailer door opens with the arrival of her mother and Norm.

"Gayle! What's the matter with you? you're standing with no clothes on in the living-room!" Cherysh shrieks.

Glancing over her shoulder Gayle simply shrugs saying: "It's not like you guys haven't seen me naked before."

Her mother's voice drops to an angry whisper of *what?* just as Norm says *Gayle...* in a warning tone. Grinning, Gayle turns to face the two of them her voice faking surprise as she says: "Oh dear! you mean you didn't know about us, Mom?"

"It was once, just once!" Norm exclaims just as Cherysh winds him with a strong punch.

Turning to her daughter she hisses: "And you can get out and take all your trashy crap with you because you won't be coming back."

"Why are you blaming me? He's the one you should throw out not me, I'm your daughter."

"And you've been a trial since you were born – no even before then when I found out I was pregnant at fifteen. You've been a penance and a burden your whole life, Gayle.

You're almost thirty years old and you have nothing, you're worth nothing, and you're nothing to me. I'm done with you." Cherysh is dry-eyed as she stands with her arms folded across her chest carefully watching and waiting for her oldest to get dressed, get packed, and get out.

"Fine, that's just fine you bi–" begins Gayle but before she can finish her mother manhandles her out the door. A moment later the hastily packed suitcase is tossed out after her.

Shaking in frustration Gayle angrily phones the club. "Put Solly on," she demands when her call is answered. It's already evening and moments later, when her boss is on the line, he warns *you better not be cancelling.*

Gayle answers: "If you want me to show up you're gonna have to pick me up or send an Uber." Cursing, Sol gets her address and says a car will arrive shortly.

Gayle squats down to fix the clothes jammed in her case and find something warmer to put on. Her lips twist in a sneer listening to the argument going on inside the trailer. She can't believe her mother is taking Norm's side over her own daughter. When the ride-share arrives she gets in without a backward glance.

The strip club is always busy on weekends but since tonight is a holiday the place will be crazier than usual. Last weekend's full moon, a *Super Moon* the guy on the TV called it, really brought the nuts out. Gayle hopes some of those sketchy guys come back so she can offload the stolen cocaine.

The gang of outlaws who own the Heavenly Bodies peeler bar sell booze and adult entertainment as a cover to funnel prostitutes, guns, and drugs through the venue.

The manager, Sol Stein, likes to say his workers are *artistes* but the reality is most of the exotic dancers, Gayle included, supplement their income with paid-for sex. The Covid distancing and no circulating restrictions make that difficult, but not impossible.

Having liquor service end at a much earlier hour actually stimulates an increase in the illicit activities. No one wants to go home just yet so private parties break out in the back rooms and even the parking lot.

Sol officially closes the club at the earlier hour, as mandated, but money is earned and payoffs are made while drinks and drugs flow freely. Little pill packets of *oxy-on-steroids* – aka fentanyl, a drug 100 times more potent than oxycodone – are freely distributed.

Last night Gayle was tipped a few pills and figures she'll sell those along with the cocaine once she finds a buyer for it. She's got to unload the coke before the owners discover their loss which means she doesn't have a lot of time.

She knows she's taken a real risk by stealing from the gang but she couldn't resist when the opportunity fell right into her lap. *Well... not exactly,* she admits to herself, *I was snooping at the time but it sure paid off. Or at least, it will.*

The bouncers on the door act like they know something about her. Atlas smirks and Jerome curls his lip in disgust. Gayle sashays up to them and tilting her head into a thinking pose says: "Jerome that's the exact same look you get on your face when you're– oops! sorry," and dropping her voice stage-whispers: "I forgot that was supposed to be our little secret."

She fake-laughs her way through the entrance hearing Atlas saying *Oh man, tell me you didn't!* and she wonders how long it will take before Jerome's girlfriend, one of the bartenders, hears the gossip. The thought puts the chip right back on Gayle's shoulder.

She almost makes it to the dressing-room door when her arm is roughly seized and she's dragged further down the hall to the manager's office. It's Sol himself who has grabbed hold of her. Gayle has never seen him look like this with a bulging vein throbbing in his forehead on his very red face. His eyes are squinted and he exhales through his nose as loudly as an angry bull.

Frightened by the air of violence radiating from him she stutters: "Solly, what? I'm not that late and–"

"Put. It. Back!" In a hoarse voice, barely above a whisper he bites off each word.

Before Gayle can even begin to tell her lie his strong fingers are wrapped around her throat, squeezing and pressing to shut her up. In the same venomous tone he repeats the three words then brutally shoves her out his office door.

Coughing and holding her hand to cover her throat Gayle hurries down the hall away from this suddenly dangerous man. Somehow he knows she's stolen from him, and she has to return the cocaine to its original hiding spot. Is he giving her a reprieve? or will he tell the club owners regardless? Gayle starts to shake at the thought of what those men will do to her. Death isn't the worst thing that can happen.

Stumbling into the dressing-room she bumps into *Kitty Kat* who curses and snarls: "Watch where you're going, slut!" Pushing past, the dancer turns back to warn: "And keep your sticky fingers off my stuff or I'll break them. I'm sick of putting up with you."

Other voices chime in *that's right!* and *same goes for me!* but Gayle ignores them. She has far more serious concerns than accusations about a missing bracelet or a pack of smokes.

Gayle is deeply distracted by her worries. As she works through her first set her movements are no more than mechanical. The patrons don't notice because she still gets her usual amount of tips. She doesn't care what they think anyhow, it's not like she's going to be sticking around this place much longer.

In between their stage performances the women work the crowd offering lap dances and more. Gayle manages to rile up one of the dancers and her client but Sol smooths things over.

Customers buy Gayle drinks, pass her a joint, and give her pills. The effects soothe Gayle's earlier fear which now morphs into angry resentment.

Vowing to herself *I'll fix that Solly. Who does he think he is? I'll show 'em all* she decides to skip her final set.

Gayle slips out of the building where she's spotted by a couple of smokers who make lewd comments and snigger. She marches straight up to them and demands a cigarette. Her belligerence earns her a smoke, a light, and the offer to snort a line. Without a thank you she turns away and heads to the cab stand, the heels of her boots click-clacking in the quiet of the night.

One of the drivers breaks away from their gossipy huddle and opening the back door of his car tells her: "You can't smoke in the taxi."

Gayle drags deeply on her cigarette before flicking it away. She doesn't exhale the smoke until she's already climbed into her seat, and is now sitting in a nicotine-smelling fog. The driver shakes his head and slams the door shut behind her.

Gayle has managed to offend and anger a dozen people and her night is only half over.

An Unwelcome Phone Call

Panda sees Judith's foot escaping from the duvet as an invitation to pounce. *Game on!* The kitten has her own fleecy cat-bed on the night-stand but once she wakens she believes everyone needs to get up.

"It's too early!" hisses Judith, but nevertheless she slips out of her warm bed so Grant isn't disturbed. Stepping into her slippers she heads into the kitchen to feed her cat.

"Stop trying to trip me!" she warns the hungry Panda who weaves between Judith's feet, excited by the prospect of food.

Judith has already showered and is dressed for the day when her phone rings. It's early for a call on a Saturday morning, especially with bad news, but as Principal, she's the contact to call in case of an emergency involving Edgemont School for Girls.

This unwelcome phone call is from the police, reporting that a body has been found on the school's back steps.

"A body? One of our girls?" she exclaims in a high-pitched squeal.

Grant hears the shock in her voice, not her words, and hurries into the room asking *What? what's going on?*

"Hang on a sec," Judith says into the receiver. "I'm putting you on speaker."

The caller, who Grant recognizes as the daytime dispatcher from the police station, imparts the news again.

"Acting on information received–" he begins in a monotone until Grant interrupts saying: "Munez? It's George Grant, tell me what happened."

"Oh Detective, hi. Sorry to ring up so early. We had a phone call at 06:48 claiming there was a female body lying on the steps at the back of the Edgemont School for Girls. The caller, a woman, said she was walking her dogs on the trail that runs behind the school when her and her dogs spotted the body. She saw that it was a young woman who was dead and then, it was so odd, the caller said *this is starting to look like carelessness.*"

Judith is startled into a barked laugh then gasps: "It's a quote! from that movie... umm, oh, oh, we just watched it on TV!"

Grant's eyes widen as he recalls the old costume-drama Judith wanted to see. He wasn't keen, but humoured her and ended up laughing his head off.

"*The Importance of Being Earnest*, and you're right the Judi Dench character says something about losing one um... parent, right? is a misfortune, but losing two is careless, or something like that. But what can this witness possibly... oh no! Munez, by any chance is the caller a Mrs. Kellogg?"

Judith turns to him in surprise recognizing the name. Mrs Kellogg was the dog-walker who discovered the body of Holly Lezinsky at the edge of School Woods in December of 2019.

"Yes Sir, that's her alright! How did you–"

"Lucky guess. Okay, so you dispatched a car to check it out and there is a body?"

"That's right. A Caucasian female—"

Insistent and anxious Judith interrupts demanding to know: "How old is she?"

"Oh, um, they said thirtyish. Maybe a year or two younger, it's hard to tell with a corpse. She was found deceased at that location and the patrolmen called for an ambulance–"

Grant cuts him off saying: "Thanks, Munez. We're going to head over there right now." Disconnecting the call he sees Judith's shoulders slump with relief to learn it isn't one of her students.

Looks at her white face he announces they'll take his car adding: "Get your warm coat on love, it'll be chilly standing around."

Absentmindedly she reaches into the closet to get her down-lined parka. She knew it was wishful thinking when she took it off the coat rack and hung it away. No doubt cold weather and snow will still be in the forecast until they are well into May.

On the short drive to the school Grant detours through a McDonald's drive-thru and orders six black coffees with creamer and sugar packets on the side.

The server hands over a cardboard tray with a bag for the fixings. Grant passes everything to Judith who carefully places it on the floor between her feet. She starts fumbling with a lid but Grant tells her to leave it until they get parked so she doesn't spill.

"Your hands are shaking sweetheart, and I don't want you getting burned."

"Oh that's right. There was a case where someone sued, in the States no doubt, I thought they were just clumsy or chasing after big bucks. I don't remember if it was a McDonalds? or some other chain... Turns out the person won their case because they truly were very badly burned."

Grant's eyebrows draw together in a frown of worry listening to Judith ramble. He swings into the lot at the back of the school and once parked he opens a coffee stirring in a couple of sugars and passes it to her.

"Oh no, that's too sweet for me," Judith begins, but Grant insists she needs it for the shock. The hot sugary drink brings some colour back to her cheeks and he's relieved to see Judith visibly pull herself together.

"That's my girl," he murmurs leaning over to kiss her on the lips.

"Grant! They can see us," protests Judith looking over at the two patrolmen who are watching them with interest. A third person, a female, is facing away from their car as she moves around taking photos.

He chuckles, saying: "Judith, I'm allowed to kiss my *fiancée*."

Stepping out of the car he waves the two policemen over. "Before we take a look grab yourselves a coffee, there's milk and sugar in the bag, and give me your report. Just in your own words, not in witness-stand jargon."

"Oh thank you Sir," says the red-headed one reaching for a cup and Judith looks twice at him saying: "I met you here before!"

He grins and confirms that he and his partner at the time, who has since transferred up Edmonton way, responded to the report of vandalism and theft when her car window was smashed in this very parking-lot.

"That's right, you were the cheeky one!" Judith states it matter-of-factly but Grant laughs out loud and the young man's face turns red.

The ambulance pulls in with it's lights flashing but no siren. As the EMTs get out the photographer comes over to join the group. The extra coffees are handed out and everyone takes a moment to enjoy the hot drinks while standing in the cool morning air.

"Detective, I finished my photos but if you'd like to have a look and point out any particular shots you need I'll be happy to take those for you. Just say the word," says the woman running a hand through her hair and eyeing Grant with interest.

Judith is used to Grant getting the come-ons and gulps her drink to hide her smile. Unfortunately it goes down the wrong way and she sprays forth a mouthful of coffee while choking out a cough. Grant rubs her back with a look of concern and Judith can't help but wonder if she was subconsciously pulling his attention away from the flirtatious woman.

"I'm fine!" she manages to rasp and waves him off to give the scene a onceover.

The cheeky policeman, as she'll always think of him, asks if she wouldn't mind having a look at the body as well, in the hope that maybe she can identify her.

Judith clears her throat and gives a firm nod. *I have a responsibility as Principal*, she thinks, *but this darn well wasn't in the job description.*

She walks over to the steps with the officers and paramedics. The young woman is lying on her back but there's nothing sleep-like about this death. It's immediately apparent this is a corpse with its torso twisted from a contraction or seizure, and the foamy bubbles of an overdose on its mouth.

Judith studies the face carefully but is certain, and relieved, that she's never seen the woman before. Grant's presence by her side is comforting.

"I don't know her. Sorry, but I have no idea who she is."

"It was a long-shot," states Grant. The two of them withdraw a few steps to let the ambulance workers do their job. Notations are made about the time, body temperature, and one of them checks their phone for the outside temperature.

As the body gets loaded on a stretcher the two police string up bright yellow tape reading *Caution – Police – Do Not Cross*.

"Oh! is that necessary?" asks Judith, dismayed at this evidence of a crime scene.

"Only until the investigator from the Medical Examiner's office comes down to search the area where the body lay and sift through any debris."

"Is that going to happen now?"

"Oh, we don't know about that stuff–" begins the other policeman but then one of the EMTs puts in: "I don't think so. We were told they're backed up because of staff being away for the long weekend."

"I see, well…" Looking from one patrolman to the other Judith uses her kind-but-stern Principal's voice to say: "This tape needs to be removed before the students show up on Tuesday morning."

The authoritative tone works and everyone nods.

Turning to Grant Judith explains that she's *just going to pop into the school for a minute*. She needs to reassure herself that everything is okay.

"I'll come with you," he says, then takes her arm to hold her back for a moment while he confers with the uniforms confirming that there's no indication anyone entered the school.

"No Sir. We walked around and checked that none of the windows were open or broken, and we rattled the handle of the front door, didn't want to disturb this handle here of course, and all is secure."

The older of the EMTs speaks up then saying: "Detective, we're going to head out with the body. Your men have the contents of her pockets and we've signed and sealed the evidence bags. There's no phone, wallet, or purse but there is some mail, a lighter, and an empty cigarette pack. The same brand as these butts ground out on the steps.

We all agree on a preliminary determination of death by misadventure, from an apparent drug overdose. There's no indication that anyone else was here," concludes the paramedic.

Judith shivers thinking of this woman sitting on the cold cement late last night or in the early hours of this morning, smoking all her cigarettes before getting high on that final, fatal dose.

"I guess I should use the front door and leave this area um... uncontaminated," she says uncertainly.

Grant's still got hold of her arm and now he pulls her close to his side, each enjoying the other's body warmth, as they walk around the building to the main doors at the front.

In the silence of the empty school their footsteps echo loudly on the tiled corridor floor. "It's kind of creepy, eh?" asks Grant in a teasing tone.

"No, I like it like this. Nice and quiet," replies Judith. They do a quick tour and everything is as it should be.

Opening the back door from inside Grant pokes his head out to tell the young officers that they can go back to the station and make their report. "Tell Munez I'll be in shortly, I brought Principal Taylor in my car so I'm going to take her back home first."

Watching the men quickly get in to their patrol car Judith remarks: "They're scampering off in a hurry!"

"Well you feel the cold when you're just standing around and it's worse when the corpse you're babysitting is about your own age. Aw Judith, I'm sorry you had to see that. What a way to ruin the holiday weekend."

"Yeah, I was just thinking I don't remember this in the job description," she half-heartedly jokes. Then double-checks that Grant did snib the inside door lock correctly.

"I've got to go back to the station and have a look through the victim's possessions once they're logged in. Hopefully this mail she's got will help identify her. I'll drop you off so you can go ahead without me to meet the Realtor and view those properties she's got lined up."

"No, I'm going to phone and cancel that appointment. With this happening I should be available for any parents who hear something happened and are concerned. Me being out house-hunting isn't a good look in the face of this tragedy."

"Okay sweetheart. I'm damn sorry you had to see a dead body, and that this had to happen here at your school. I'll be awhile. I have to get started working the case because even though it's an accidental death we still have to answer questions like *how did she get here?* I didn't see any other cars in the parking lot.

Oh, and I have to talk to Mrs. Kellogg again... that'll be fun."

"You can break the ice by asking her if she enjoyed *The Importance of Being Earnest*. She must have seen it the other night same as we did."

Grant smiles replying, "I agree. She didn't strike me as the type to go around quoting Oscar Wilde as a rule," He pushes the detritus of their hot drinks onto the floor at the back of the car then ushers Judith into her seat.

They make a stop on the way home and once she's back in her apartment again Judith texts Lila:

call me when u can i have news

The phone rings right away. "Judith I'm so glad to see you texting properly. Did you use your thumbs like I told you to?"

"Lila! There's no time to chat, we've got a dead body on the back steps of the school!"

"We—what?!" Lila gasps out the question.

Tucking the phone between shoulder and chin Judith starts prepping her French Press. The take-out coffee Grant bought earlier was surprisingly good, but she's craving a mugful of her own brand.

Continuing her conversation with Lila she explains: "I've just come back. The police called me since I'm the contact for the school and Grant drove me over and yeah, there's this woman – no idea who she is – lying sprawled on the steps and she's dead!"

"How did she die?"

"They think it's a drug overdose."

She can hear Lila's dismayed tut-tut sound. "Ohhh, she OD'ed on the school steps... we've never had trouble with people hanging out in the parking-lot before, have we?"

"Never, and Mr. Glover confirmed that," agrees Judith.

"He was there?"

"No, I told him. Actually I made Grant stop by his house. He's old and I didn't want him to get a shock. I know for a fact he goes to check up at the school on weekends. He's always worried about pipes bursting, or the boiler failing, or something.

The police strung that yellow *Caution!* tape all around the back entrance and Mr. Glover would have seen it for sure."

"Oh, I bet he was upset by the news." Lila states with sympathy in her voice.

"Yes, they both were. Mrs. Glover insisted on making us tea and I wasn't going to accept but Grant gestured to me for us to stay so I said *yes, please*. Of course a cup of tea involved a tray and cookies and napkins, and all of us sitting down in the living room.

Mr. Glover asked the same questions and made the same comments several times over but by time we left he was calm and his colour was back to normal.

Grant was right, the old couple needed time to deal with the shock in their own way."

"He's sensitive like that."

"Yeah, it's a nice contrast to the *macho cop type* portrayed on TV. Grant is perceptive.

I'm just making a coffee while we talk because you know I'm not much of a tea drinker. The homemade cookies were good, though.

Anyhow, Grant brought me home and I called you right away. I need to phone Samira too. Any parents who happen to see that ghastly police tape will be ringing up with questions. Of course they'll phone each other first to spread the gossip under the guise of *collecting info*, but that can't be helped. Human nature and all that."

"What can you tell me about the dead woman? I'm guessing there was no blood but were her lips blue? She wasn't sexually assaulted, was she?"

"Let me answer your questions in order. She looked to be in her mid- to late-twenties, dyed blonde hair overdue for a touch-up, she looked tall lying down, no blood, very um.. curvy and, well, tons of make-up so I couldn't see her real lip colour, oh and very revealing clothes, but everything looked intact."

"I wonder who she is?"

"And why was she there of all places?"

"Those are the questions, aren't they?"

Good Day / Bad Day

Harry lies in bed feeling weak and worn out after spending what felt like half the night hugging the toilet. *Without even getting drunk first,* he thinks. *No fun, totally unfair.* Instead he'd been vomiting the dregs of the gasoline he'd siphoned into his car. His tongue feels burnt. The skin around his mouth is red and irritated.

What started out as the best day of his life ended in the misery of a sick stomach.

It began with his kid sister Didi. She's thrilled to have gotten a place on the Track Team at her school, the Edgemont School for Girls, and had begged him to come time her as she practised.

"You said you don't have to go to work today so you can come with me. The school's closed for the long weekend so nobody's gonna be around to watch and make fun of me."

"I thought things were better at this school you go to now?" he asks, immediately riled by the thought of Didi being bullied.

"Oh it is, it's like a million times better. 'Cause mostly it was boys who picked on me and we don't have any here."

It's not surprising that Didi caught the attention of her male classmates. Her mixed-race heritage resulted in big brown eyes with naturally thick, dark lashes; full pouty lips; and smooth caramel-coloured skin. Even at thirteen her long-legged figure is shapely, and in five years she'll be a stunning young woman. Harry was so relieved when she got accepted into the subsidized programme at the local all-girls school.

Each of Cherysh Boudreau's three children have a different father. She only married once, but she made sure each child's Dad was named on the birth certificate. So Gayle, the eldest, is a Boudreau. Harry's surname is Drapeau, another of Cherysh's French-Canadian lovers; and Didi's father, Dante Jackson, is Black. He's the only one who is still around, and Harry figures it means he never stopped loving Cherysh.

Dante was always good to both Didi and Harry when they were growing up. If he took Didi to the Calgary Zoo or ice-skating at Olympic Plaza he'd always invite Harry to come along as well.

He never liked Gayle though. At seventeen years older she could be Didi's mother but she's never shown any interest in her baby sister. Until recently, that is. In the few days she's been back living at home Gayle was putting make-up on Didi and trying different hairstyles on the girl. Harry didn't like it. He's never trusted Gayle, she only cares about herself.

So here he is spending his Saturday afternoon at the schoolyard to watch Didi race around the cinder track. The sight of the yellow crime scene tape brings them both to a standstill.

"Look! What's this all about? It's just like TV! Do you see anything?" Didi asks, as they slowly edge closer to the back steps of the school.

"Like what? like blood or something?"

"Harry, eww!" she squeals but her face is alight with curiosity. The tape starts at the side of the door, stretches down along the hand-railing then across the bottom of the steps and back up the other side. The brother and sister look closely but there's nothing to see.

"C'mon, there's nothing here, and I'm sure you can still use the track," Harry says, dragging Didi to the playing field.

She takes one last glance at the steps and gives an exaggerated shiver exclaiming: "Somebody just walked on my grave!"

"Your grave, huh? Well I guess that means you're seeing really far into the future since you're just a kid and your death is a long way off."

Indignantly Didi declares: "I'm not a kid! and besides, it's just an expression."

She then effortlessly scissors her legs into the splits and reaching from one ankle to the next does a few stretching exercises before jumping to her feet and getting out on the track. Didi is an incredibly fast runner. It's why she made the team even though the rest of the girls are all older.

Despite being proud and impressed by his athletic sister Harry is resigned to the boredom of hanging around watching. *But my good deed has paid off,* he congratulates himself, *because I get to talk to Bethany Penner.*

Beth had also come out to practise today, just finishing up when they arrived, and decided she'd stay to visit with Harry and watch Didi, too.

After the exercise Beth's colour is fresh and even without any make-up on she is radiant with healthy good looks. Harry doesn't think in those terms – his senses, mind, and body simply react to the presence of a pretty girl.

The two of them speculate about the police tape with Beth saying she'll ask Lila, her Dad's girlfriend who is also the School Nurse, about it. *No one was up when I left this morning so I never heard any news, but Lila will find out what happened,* she says with confidence.

Didi interrupts one of her laps to come over and say *hi Beth* and ask if she'll watch her run. Beth is kind to his hero-worshipping sister and that makes Harry feel good. He wouldn't know it, but Beth Penner is a favourite of all the younger students at Edgemont School for Girls.

"Sure, I'll watch you Didi, and if I have any suggestions I'll let you know," Beth said, much to his sister's delight.

So she and Harry stand side-by-side for about five minutes before he mentions that they'll be more comfortable on the bleachers and Beth agrees to sit and hang out for a bit.

Afterwards he can't remember what they talked about, he was too distracted thinking how *her whole face lights up when she laughs.* He wants to keep making her laugh so he teases and jokes and clowns around.

The sun has come out and warmed the air and Harry suddenly experiences the joy of being young and alive. The rays highlight the red in Beth's hair and he finds himself thinking *this is what they mean when they talk about someone's hair being strawberry-blonde.*

Once Didi has finally worn herself out she and Harry walk Beth home.

"What are you guys doing for Easter?"

"My Dad is taking me to a restaurant and he told me to wear a nice dress so it must be a fancy place. I told him Gayle, she's my big sister, has been showing me how to put on make-up but he said *no, I can't wear any because he doesn't like it.*"

Harry volunteers that he and Didi have different fathers, but his isn't around anymore so he won't be doing anything special for the holiday.

"Well, would you like to have dinner with us? My soon-to-be stepmother, who I was telling you about, is cooking a feast and told me I can invite a friend if I want." Seeing the wistful look on Didi's face she tactfully adds: "We won't be dressing up for a special occasion like Didi is, but Lila's a great cook so, what do you say?"

Harry is tongue-tied and struggles to answer but luckily Didi is ready to accept on his behalf. "He'll come for sure, won't you Harry? I'd have come too but I can't disappoint my Dad."

Gravely Beth agrees that that would never do. She puts her number in Harry's phone and texts herself so she'll have his. "There! we're all set and this is my place here so now you know where I live.

Dinner's early, at 4:00, so we'll see you then, okay?" Harry grins and manages to thank Beth for the invite.

Didi chatters, skips, and dances all the way home. Harry is so wrapped up in his happy thoughts of Bethany he simply drifts along. *Like I'm floating on air*, he chuckles, making fun of himself.

Arriving at their trailer he just stands staring stupidly at the space where his car should be. Nobody would have stolen his Ford Focus, it's just about as old as he is. The car had already had several owners before he got it. *So where...?*

He hears his big sister hollering inside the trailer and immediately knows she's had something to do with his car disappearing. Yanking the front door open he's ready for a fight but Gayle beats him to it.

"That garbage car of yours left me stranded!" she complains. Before Harry can utter a word she locks herself in the bathroom and turns on the shower. Harry's left standing with his hands fisted and an angry tirade boiling inside.

Her angry dismissal of him leaves Harry fuming and stuttering to get the words out but luckily Didi reminds him it's a long weekend and he can't waste time fighting with Gayle. She's right, an abandoned car will attract all kinds of mischief tonight.

Harry doesn't complain when Didi tags along, she's better off keeping her distance from their older sister anyhow. They don't have to walk far before he spots his car.

He can see some sort of official paper stuck on the windshield already. The police who patrol Edgemont are very efficient and he's lucky it wasn't towed away.

It's an *Abandoned Vehicle Notice* stating the car is deemed to be worthless and if not removed within 72 hours will be transported, at the owner's expense, to a salvage yard or municipal dump for disposal.

Harry mutters a curse because his car certainly isn't worthless to him. He needs his spare key and goes to fish out the metal keybox stuck behind the back wheel-well when Didi states: "The keys are still in the car."

"What? She just left them in the ignition!" Harry is indignant but when he gets in and turns on the power he sees the flashing E over the gas-pump icon. The car isn't going anywhere without fuel. It won't even start.

"Didi I'm gonna phone Paul to get him to come pick me up so I can go to a gas station."

Twisting his hips he pulls out his wallet and is reminded again of how little money he has. Before he can even ask his sister tells him: "Gayle got into my Pokemon piggy-bank and took my twenty dollars dog-walking money. But I've got some loonies and toonies you can have..."

"No keep your money but thanks, sis. I want you to go before Paul gets here." As her face falls he immediately feels badly, especially since she just offered him the last of her funds, so he tries to explain.

"Didi, you know Paul isn't exactly a good guy and he thinks you're *hot* which makes me want to punch him in the face even if he is my best friend."

Didi giggles as she tells Harry she thinks Paul is *totally bleech* and makes a vomiting sound to go with her comment. Harry gives a genuine laugh at her antics. He's reminded just how young 13-year-old Didi is, her behaviour swinging wildly from kiddie to teenager and back again.

Paul has been ogling Didi for over a year now. He never misses an opportunity to compliment her unusual colouring, or remark that her body is filling out nicely. Her height makes her look older, too. Harry doesn't like it one little bit but he realizes Didi is safer sticking with him rather than walking home alone now that it's turned dark.

"Okay but just ignore him if he says anything, and if he tries to touch you you tell me right away, okay?"

"If he touches me I'll deck him!" the young girl asserts.

Smiling, despite his worries, Harry calls his friend and explains the situation. "That's hilarious, Harry. Your big sister is such a bitch! but listen, I'm already out so I can be there in like five minutes."

"Can you stop and get some gas for me? I've got fifteen bucks–"

"That's no good, they'll want a $20 deposit just for the gas can, maybe more, so we'll just have to siphon. I keep a bit of hose in the trunk just in case but you've got to do it because I don't want to be puking gas all night."

"Sure I'll do it, but you're not supposed to drink it, you know."

Paul's laugh is a guffaw. "Yeah? you've never siphoned gas if you think you can do it without swallowing some. It's gonna be fun watching you, Harry."

Ending the call Harry turns to his sister and reminds her again: "Remember what I said about keeping your distance from Paul."

"But he's your best friend, Harry," Didi asks, her confusion showing plainly. Harry sighs deeply. He's never been good at finding the right words to explain things.

"Look Dee, all I can tell you is sometimes you meet people who you like even though you know they're no good. But they're fun to hang out with so you just keep them separate from the rest of your life, or something, I don't know how to say it. I like Paul, but I don't want you liking him, so just trust me, okay?"

Didi idolizes her brother so of course it's okay, whatever he says will always be okay with her, even though she doesn't understand.

Paul arrives soon after with a long length of good hose. At Harry's questioning look Paul smirks, commenting *sometimes I need gas and I don't have any cash so...* When Harry shakes his head Paul just shrugs.

After positioning his car as closely as he can to Harry's Ford Paul steps back to give instruction on the process of suctioning up gasoline. Harry has to draw it from Paul's tank before ripping the hose end from his mouth and pushing it into his tank. After a few back and forths he manages to get enough gas into his car but not without lots of gagging and spitting.

Didi is ready to cry, but Paul has a good laugh. He pulls her close with an arm around her shoulders but she slips out from under and stands well away.

"Hey! What's your problem, little girl?"

"You're being mean, Paul. It's not funny, Harry is getting sick."

"I'm okay, Sis but get in the car, we'll head straight home. Paul man, thanks for this but I kinda hate you right now."

Paul laughs loudly and taking back his hose coils it up ready for use again. He follows Harry's car back to their trailer but instead of pulling in he beeps his horn as a goodbye and keeps driving.

During the short trip Harry has thrown up all over himself. He doesn't want to chance stopping the car in case it won't start again. Didi doesn't complain, she just opens the window to give him fresh air and clear away the smell. Once they're home she runs to open the door for Harry.

Norm is just heading out to work his night shift and one look at his scowling face is enough for both kids to only nod at him without speaking.

Their mother sits at the kitchen table with a mug of coffee and a full ashtray. Her eyes are suspiciously red but neither of her children have ever seen her cry. They know the adults have been fighting and figure it's best to just keep out of the way.

Cherysh frowns over the mess Harry's clothes are in but doesn't question him and neither of the kids volunteer an explanation.

Didi follows Harry to his room, leaning in the doorway as he flops down on his bed with a groan. He drags the metal wastebasket to the side of his bed.

"Are you gonna be okay?" she asks.

"Yeah I will, but I've got to do something about Gayle. She's gone too far this time, I could have lost my car!" he angrily exclaims. Clenching his fists he tells Didi: "I'm gonna kill her."

"I'll help," the young girl promises. "I'm gonna get on my school chat and see if anybody knows why that yellow tape is there."

She takes a last look at her pale, shaky brother before leaving him to recover.

After a bad night Harry does manage to get some sleep but wakens early still feeling nauseous. Lying there he lets his mind replay the perfect day he'd had before coming home to his missing car.

That memory makes his stomach clench again so he calms himself by thinking about seeing Beth again in a couple of days.

Identifying the Body

In the early hours of April 3rd Cherysh Boudreau gives up trying to sleep and heads into the kitchen to make herself a cup of coffee. She's already spent most of the night tossing and turning so the caffeine won't make things worse.

She moves quietly since her two youngest are sleeping. This trailer has been her home for a dozen years so she doesn't need to turn on a light to find her way around. Popping in a coffee pod and waiting for the machine to dispense her coffee Cherysh takes a cigarette from her pack, ready to light it when she has her drink in hand.

While waiting she glances out the window over the sink. There is solar lighting alongside the roadway so the grounds are never totally dark.

When Cherysh first moved here the couple running the place couldn't care less about anyone's safety and at night the trailer park was pitch black. After they retired – to the relief of all the residents – Jerry Bennett, a trailer owner himself, applied for the Manager position and has done a great job ever since.

The glowing lights required only a minimal cash outlay and were easily set-up but they've made a real difference to the feel and comfort of the place.

As her eyes become accustomed to the dim light Cherysh spots Norm's car. Just as she starts thinking *why would his car be here?* she realizes he must be sleeping in it.

That idiot! she thinks, and grabbing someone's raincoat from the hooks by the door she hurries outside.

Looking in the window she can see Norm lying on the reclined driver's seat with his legs stretched over the gear shift and across the passenger seat. Pausing to study his face she notices how smooth his skin is when he sleeps. Awake, Norm's eyes are crinkled from his constant smiling. He's a happy man and his face is always animated and expressive.

She lightly raps on the glass making him jump. Cherysh doesn't speak in case any of her neighbours are still up and ready to eavesdrop but he gets the message when she jerks her head back towards her trailer.

Norm is so stiff he practically falls out of his vehicle and Cherysh thinks *serves him right for buying that little sports car.*

Inside the trailer Norm pulls Cherysh into his arms with a grateful, soul-deep sigh. She relaxes into his embrace for a minute but when he starts apologizing she pushes him off to the bedroom to go sleep.

She and Norm hooked up on a blind date and next thing she knew they were in a relationship. He isn't even her usual type, he's far too nice of a guy. But his calm presence is soothing, and she knows she'll forgive him. Gayle was never anything but trouble.

Leaning against her kitchen counter Cherysh puts out her smoke half-way through and finishes her coffee in a couple of gulps. Her thoughts are all over the place but finally she just shakes her head at herself and follows Norm into her room.

It's about seven hours later when the two detectives, Grant and his partner Reg Osborne, come knocking at Cherysh's door. It's one of her rules to never invite police inside her home but when they start explaining the purpose of their visit she ushers them in.

Cherysh keeps them standing in the entryway while the handsome one tells her a young woman's body was found outside Edgemont School for Girls and the mail she had in her pocket was addressed to this residence.

"Someone has my mail?"

"Yes, it's a Costco cheque, the envelope was opened, and sent to this address so–"

"That's my rebate!" exclaims Cherysh.

Looking at the voucher Grant says: "It's made out to C. Boudreau–"

An indignant Cherysh grabs it from his hand fuming: "That's me. This is mine. Who's stealing my mail?"

Grant holds back the retort that the dead woman isn't stealing anything from any one any more. "So, you are C Boudreau, what does the C stand for?"

"Cherysh," she says twisting her lips at the fanciful name. "That's Cherysh with a y not an i," she tells Reg seeing him write in his notepad.

The detectives wait for Cherysh's questions. But she doesn't ask anything. The three of them remain in the doorway with Cherysh seemingly lost in thought.

A voice calls: "Cherysh? Who's here?" and a tall, middle-aged Asian man steps into the short hallway.

"It's the police, Norm. They've come to tell me some woman is dead and she had my Costco rebate cheque in her pocket."

The man is understandably confused but Cherysh doesn't pay attention to his surprised look, she's already turned back to Grant demanding: "So who is she? and you didn't say how she died. What happened?"

"The Medical Examiner will pronounce on cause of death–" begins Grant but seeing anger on the woman's face at being fobbed off he quickly adds: "Apparently it's a drug overdose. But Ms. Boudreau do you know a young woman, approximately 5′ 8″ or 9″ in her late twenties who would have your mail on her?"

"Cherysh, it must be Gayle!" exclaims the man.

"Naw, I threw her out yesterday and she knows better than to come back." The two of them exchange a look, both recalling that Cherysh threw Norm out as well but here he is back in her trailer again.

"Besides, Gayle didn't do drugs. At least... not that I know of and I wouldn't have thought it. Except why would she be at that school? She never went there. But who knows why Gayle does any of the things she does. Frankly, there's nothing my daughter won't get up to."

"It's possible this woman is your daughter?" blurts out Reg in surprise. Silently he thinks *she sure doesn't look old enough to have a kid that age.*

She cocks an eyebrow and gives him a sardonic look replying: "Child bride. I had Gayle when I was fifteen and stupid. Stupid to get pregnant and even stupider to marry her no-good father."

"So the deceased might be your daughter whose name is Gayle Boudreau?"

"I guess it could be her... I suppose I've got to come with you to take a look? I've seen that on TV shows."

"Yes, but not immediately. With the long weekend the Medical Examiner's office is short-staffed and they won't have the body ready to view yet."

Grant is relieved he doesn't have a wailing, sobbing mother to deal with but this coldness is... unsettling. Still, it does makes his job easier. "I have some photos if I could show them to you?"

Cherysh folds her arms across her chest and nods. Reg opens the file folder he's carrying and passes over a couple of pictures. Cherysh studies them in silence and Norm leans over her shoulder to have a look as well.

"That's her!" he says in a shocked whisper, wrapping his arms around Cherysh.

She accepts his hug but her only comment is: "Yeah, it's Gayle all right. Look at those boots! she always liked flashy stuff. Even as a young girl she was vain. But... what a lousy way to die."

A beautiful young girl hurries down the hall towards them asking: "Mom? What's going on?" and an exasperated Cherysh shoos everyone into her living-room.

She tells the girl that Gayle has died and the teen immediately bursts into tears. Then another teenager appears, a boy about sixteen or seventeen, and he puts his arm around his sister in a protective manner.

Neither Grant nor Reg take a seat as they watch Cherysh explain that Gayle took drugs and died. The youth's face is white with shock and after a startlingly loud burp he turns and flees back down the hall.

"What's up with your brother?" demands Cherysh.

"He had to siphon gas into his car last night and he's been throwing up ever since. I think he swallowed a bunch of it."

"Oh great Didi, the cops are here and you're telling them Harry is stealing gas?"

"He didn't steal it, he's not a thief!" the young girl is offended on her brother's behalf. "Paul let him take it, he even gave Harry the hose to use."

"Miss, that's an extremely dangerous thing to do! The vapours can burn and if the gasoline enters the lungs it can even cause death." Reg expostulates. Didi looks ready to start crying again.

Grant pieces together the story and confirms it with the girl who is introduced as Didi, Didi Jackson, Gayle's thirteen-year-old sister. Her brother is called Harry Drapeau and he's seventeen. Didi volunteers that Gayle only just moved back home a few days ago and has been sleeping on the couch.

"When's the last time you saw your daughter, Ms. Boudreau?"

"Early evening, yesterday, we'd just come home and she was getting ready to go to work. It must have been about seven? when a car came and picked her up." Nothing in Cherysh's face or voice hinted at the fight she'd had with her daughter or her boyfriend.

"You mentioned you threw her out?"

"Yeah, I told her I wanted some rent money by the first but she hadn't paid me anything. Plus, she was fighting with her brother and sister so when she left for work I told her to not to come back. She took her suitcase so I figured she had some place to sleep at last night."

"Where did Gayle work?"

Cherysh sarcastically replied that her daughter was an exotic dancer who worked at *Heavenly Bodies* as *Lady L'Amour*. "It's a peeler bar and God knows what she did to hustle tips. Gayle worked there for a few years, which is longer than she's held down any other job. She dropped out of school as soon as she could so it's not like she had a lot of options."

"Heavenly Bodies?" asks Reg. Turning to Grant he explains: "The Calgary Drug Squad raided that place late last night. They gave the station a courtesy call to let us know *they were conducting a warranted search based on information received.* They didn't need any assistance from us."

"We'll get in touch with them and find out what happened. Ms. Boudreau Didi mentioned that Gayle's been sleeping here for a few nights, can you tell me where she was before then?"

"Norm? What was the name of that guy Gayle was shacked up with? Remember we ran into them when we'd gone out for drinks one night."

The man, Norm presumably since he hadn't been introduced, answers: "Eric Littner. He's a really nice guy. We got talking and he said he owns an office supply company, it's a franchise, in Calgary. He even gave me a card that's good for a 25% discount off anything in his store."

Reg asks if he still has the card and Norm leaves the room to fetch it. "I'll want it back," he says as he hands it over.

Reg explains that he doesn't need to keep the card, he'll just copy down the contact information. That's what he says, but what he actually does is photograph it with his phone.

Belatedly Norm invites the detectives to sit down but Grant says they'll be heading out now. "Just to re-cap, you last saw Gayle about 7:00 pm when she got a ride presumably taking her to her job at Heavenly Bodies, and you weren't expecting her back last night, correct?"

"Yeah, that's right."

"What were all of you doing last night? Besides siphoning gas," he says with a smile towards Didi. Despite her young age she has the typical female reaction to Grant and grins back.

"Me and Harry had just gotten home about then but we didn't talk to Gayle, she went straight into the shower hogging the bathroom as usual.

I was mad at her for stealing my babysitting money and Harry was mad at her for taking his car and leaving it on the road."

Grant asks: "This is the same car that needed gas?" just as Cherysh demands the story behind the stolen dog-walking money.

Answering her mother first Didi says: "She took everything I had, a whole twenty dollars that I'd saved from walking Mrs. Frobisher's Daisy."

Turning back to Grant she continues: "Yeah, it was on *empty*. I guess that's why she left it. She even left the keys in the ignition!" Didi is offended by this disregard for her brother's property. "Harry went to bed because he felt sick and I chatted with my girlfriends online. Oh! Did you put that yellow tape over the back steps at the school?"

Cherysh scowls at her daughter and nudges her out of the living-room and back down the hallway.

Answering Grant's question she tells him: "Norm and I didn't go out again once we got home so we were here all night too," states Cherysh before adding dismissively, "So you'll let me know when I have to go do this identifying the body thing, right?"

Reg turns to another page in his notebook and getting Cherysh's phone number tells her *we'll send a car but I'll phone you first*. Looking into her eyes his gaze is full of sympathy, but he's met with an impassive stare masking any emotion.

Reg silently tut-tuts not realizing that Cherysh Boudreau's insides are in a turmoil as she struggles with a confusion of thoughts.

Living for much of her youth on the precarious edge of danger Cherysh learned self-control as a necessity. She hasn't had an easy time of it.

Tracing Gayle's Movements

Leaving the trailer park Grant and Reg head back to their office to contact the drug squad in Calgary for details of the arrest warrant and to find out what came of it.

On the way they discuss the Boudreau household. "Even though it's unofficial I'm prepared to proceed on the basis that we've ID'ed the body. I can't believe I'm complaining about no hysterics but seriously? how can Ms. Cherysh Boudreau, the victim's mother, be so cold?"

"A hard-hearted woman, that's for sure. But we can't judge, Grant. We don't know what her life has been like. Pregnant and unhappily married at fifteen? That's not a good start."

"No, not for her or her baby daughter."

"At least she seems to be taking care of the two kids she's got at home," comments Ray.

"Yeah, it could be that Gayle was just... trouble."

"Speaking of trouble they're gonna have their hands full when that little beauty Didi finishes growing."

Grant chuckles in agreement adding that he likes her brother Harry, who seems to be in protective mode already.

Once they're settled in the office Grant calls the Calgary Drug Squad and is relieved to speak to an officer called Collins, not his ex-partner Suzanne Mirteau, although he does enquire after her.

"Oh Detective Mirteau didn't last long here. With her looks? she got snapped up right away into some Public Relations position."

"Why? She's a decorated police officer with years of experience and great interviewing skills–"

But Collins interrupts to say: "She chose this promotion, and the big salary that comes with it. Her photo is all over the force's infomercials, recruitment, social media, you name it. It was a good move for Mirteau because just between you and me, well if you two used to be partners you'll know all about it anyhow, but she was hard to work with and there were complaints. She was very um... flirtatious. And demanding, too."

"Yeah, that definitely sounds familiar," Grant answers with a sigh. "Oh well, I hope things work out for her in this new direction her career has taken."

"She sure is a beautiful woman. Were you two ever... uh, you know?"

"I do know and no, we never were. First off, I was her superior and work relationships get messy. Plus it didn't take long to discover what a possessive, jealous woman Suzanne is. I have no compunction talking about her because I'm quite sure she spread plenty of stories about me. I'll always take the chance to clear the air whenever I can."

"You're right Grant," the other man says with a wry chuckle. "Mirteau had plenty to say about you and other than the fact that apparently you look like a male model none of it was good."

"Collins I'm really not sure if male model is good either!" Grant laughs back with mock outrage. "Actually, Suzanne did her best to come between me and my girl so no, there's no love lost between us. Anyhow, I won't be seeing her now that she's moved up into the establishment admin so good luck and good riddance."

"Yeah, so long as she doesn't end up being Chief some day."

Grant splutters out the mouthful of coffee he'd just swallowed which sets Reg off into gales of laughter.

"I'm Reg Osborne, Collins, and thanks for giving me my laugh for the day. You're on speaker, by the way. Grant here is dripping coffee and it's hilarious. I never met Suzanne Mirteau but now I want to!" Reg chuckles some more before explaining why they're phoning.

"I just got the report on that ten minutes ago and I was going to give you guys a call. You saved me looking up your number. Anyhow it was a bit of a damp squib, I mean we did collect about a kilo of cocaine – good stuff too – but we weren't able to make an arrest."

"How did you get onto it?"

"We got an anonymous tip. A female called it in about 23:30 saying we'd find a stash of hard drugs in a dressing-room locker that was going to be moved out that night. So, some urgency. The Crown expedited a warrant and we opened all the lockers. We only found drugs in the one but the girl who uses it wasn't there to arrest.

You'll be getting an APB on a Gayle, that's-with-a-y, Boudreau, a stripper who worked at Heavenly Bodies under the name *Lady L'Amour*–"

"Save your manpower, Collins, Gayle Boudreau overdosed last night and she's dead. She spelled her name with a y, eh?"

"That's what we were told—"

Reg interrupts to point out it's the same way Cherysh spells her name.

"Well, I expect she's the one who named her daughter and spelled it out for the birth certificate."

'Okay I don't know what you guys are talking about but your news is... wow. I wonder if she's the tipster?"

"Why would she inform on herself? Unless... unless she planned on taking a big dose of the drug and it's a suicide not an accident. Hmm maybe, but the EMTs told us the drug was fentanyl, not cocaine."

"Maybe she did it to cause some trouble?" Reg surmises.

"Some trouble, but not much. We cited the club manager for violating Covid hours of operation and capacity restrictions, for serving alcohol after hours, and found a couple of people openly using drugs but they didn't have enough product to get them arrested.

We spotted a known pill dealer but he slipped out the moment we came through the door and he got away. So all we're left with are minor charges, just nuisance stuff, and the club will be open again tonight."

Collins sounds discouraged so Reg reminds him that he also took illegal drugs off the street and cost some trafficker $20-plus grand.

"Yeah you're right, some lowlife is out-of-pocket and that's a good thing."

Grant tells Collins they were told Gayle was going to the club at about 19:00 hours and asks if the report can shed any light on her movements.

"Oh sure. This *Lady L'Amour* was at the club, she danced her first set and then *worked the floor* as the manager put it, but she skipped out before her second act. Of course my men didn't know she died later that night and their questions were about dealing, stuff like who are her friends? where she might have gone? you know.

Seems like there was nobody close to her, or not saying so if they were, 'cause we didn't get any answers. No one remembers seeing Gayle Boudreau after 22:00 but no one will swear to it."

"Okay thanks Tom – I'm guessing that's what they call you, eh?"

"Oh yeah, I've been Tom Collins for so long I sometimes forget my name is Brandon."

The three of them chuckle and end their call.

"So..." Grant pauses to think a moment. "If we assume Gayle left the club between 10:00 and 10:15, and phoned in the tip about 11:30 then where was she during that missing hour-and-a-half?"

"And if she took an Uber or Lyft to work that night, how did she get to wherever it was she went?"

"We need to check out the club's surveillance feed for the exits and find out."

"Saturday night at the peeler bar. Oh well, someone's gotta do it," says Reg with a grin.

"And it's Easter long weekend so they'll be busy. Oh! I wonder if the girls will be dressed up as bunnies? I mean like Playboy bunnies," clarifies Grant.

"Well duh! I wouldn't expect anyone wanting to see these girls wearing fuzzy onesies that cover them from head to toe!"

"With that crowd? You never know," answers Grant darkly.

Reg smirks and looking at his watch says, "The club won't be open for hours."

"Yeah, I'm going home to have some dinner and let's meet up there at... 10:00 pm suit you?"

"Yeah, we'll be able to ruin their plans of staying open longer than allowed."

"And that will still be within a 24-hour cycle for the video, of course it might be stored in the cloud anyhow."

"I doubt it. These types of places don't like having permanent records if they can avoid it."

"That's true. Well, I have to explain to Judith how I'll be spending my night – any tips?"

"As a divorced man my advice – hindsight being 20-20, as they say – is always tell the truth. Besides, I'm sure Judith will understand how serious this is. After all, somebody sold or gave Gayle Boudreau a deadly dose of a recreational drug."

***

Handsome George Grant could pass for a lawyer, banker, or any type of businessman, but Reg Osborne's appearance says cop through-and-through. Both men are big with Reg, the elder of the two, carrying solid bulk.

As they approach the strip club one of the bouncers looks ready to question them but a nudge from the other guy silences him. The two detectives enter a busy, noisy room that's rowdy with drinkers and dancers partying.

"Covid restrictions are right out the window with this crowd," exclaims Reg. All of the proximity rules, number of people, table spacing, dancing, masking, and drinking regulations are blatantly ignored.

A stern-faced Grant nods in agreement stating: "It's a mockery. Obviously the fines aren't slowing them down, just another cost of doing business, I guess."

"They should be shut down!"

"Right now we're only here to get the surveillance video but I'll take this to the Chief and hopefully she'll be able to do that."

As the men make their way across the room to the bar their progress is noted. Some of the conversations stop altogether, while negotiations with the women working the audience are paused.

The redheaded bartender smiles a greeting as they approach and both men struggle to keep their eyes on her face and off her impressive cleavage. Grant can only imagine the lewd comments and crude propositions she gets throughout her working day and hopes the tips are worth it.

"Hello. I'm Detective Grant and this is Detective Osborne. Can you call the Manager to come speak with us, please?"

"Sure, Jolene's doing that now," she nods towards the far end of the bar where a blonde is on the house phone. "I'm Rusty, and what can I get for you while you wait? It's on the house."

"We're good Rusty, but thanks." While Grant talks to the bartender Reg is casting a professional eye around the room causing a few patrons to quickly finish their drinks and leave.

A neatly dressed man in early middle-age strides towards them announcing himself: "Evening Officers, I'm Solomon Stein, the Club Manager. We already had a visit from the police last night so... what can I do for you two?"

Drawing the man to a quieter corner away from listeners Grant explains what they need. Since Stein is pursing his lips and looking ready to refuse their request Grant elaborates.

"I can tell you this because the next-of-kin has already been notified... obviously it's bad news. Your employee Gayle Boudreau, aka *Lady L'Amour*, was found dead from an apparent drug overdose in the early hours of Saturday," he breaks off at the manager's shocked look.

"Gayle? Dead? I can't believe it. She was just here last night and she was fine–"

"That's why we want to take the video to study."

"But Gayle isn't a user. Honestly I can't believe she's died from an overdose."

"As I said, we need to trace her movements: who she had contact with here and what happened after she left. You do have cameras inside the club and on the doors, right?"

"We do but... our customers have the right to enjoy our entertainment without having their privacy violated–"

This time it's Reg who interrupts stating: "You have a sign posted on the door warning that video surveillance is operating. Anyone who chooses to enter is implicitly agreeing to being recorded."

"Well, yeah but... I still don't think I can release that to you. I'll need to contact the owners who will probably want to take legal advice."

"Look, Mr. Stein, if someone here passed a tainted drug to Ms. Boudreau we need to know about it asap before they can harm anyone else. On the other hand if the feed doesn't show anything like that then we'll know the drug didn't originate from this Club."

"As I'm sure you're aware the Drug Squad busted in here last night and raided the dancers' dressing-room, opening, and in one case even breaking open, the girls' lockers. In Gayle's they found a quantity of cocaine but there were no other drugs anywhere else. Still, it's an added complication so no, I don't think I can release that video to you. Not until I get clearance from my boss."

"Can we at least look at the video from when Gayle left? We hope we'll see if she spoke to anyone, or if anyone followed her out, or what kind of car she got in to. We understand she didn't have a car of her own?"

"She did, but it got repossessed. Right out of our lot here," he shakes his head over the unpleasant memory. "I remember because Gayle caused a scene with her swearing and crying when the tow-truck picked it up. I couldn't help her, she'd leased a sporty Audi and the payments were astronomical."

Sol thinks quietly for a couple of minutes and Grant is just about to speak when the manager says: "Here's what I can do. I'll let you see the outside video from when Gayle left which must have been close to 10:30."

"How do you know that?"

"She was supposed to do her second set at 10:30 but she never showed up. We checked for her everywhere and she was definitely not here in the Club. Her first dance was at 9:00, she was a bit late which was usual for Gayle, and after she finished I saw her working the floor before going back to the dressing-room to change into her second costume. I fully expected to see her on that stage shortly after that.

Anyhow, yes to seeing the outside video, but the inside video will have to wait for now."

Grant and Reg exchange a wordless communication. It's been their experience that the province's Privacy Laws seem to serve as nothing more than an excuse to avoid responsibility. They've been thwarted by the Act before. They agree that something is better than nothing and ask to view the video from outside.

The time stamp reads 22:14 when Gayle is seen walking away from the front door. They watch her interaction with the smokers then see her march up to the first cab that's in the line. The driver can be seen saying something as he opens the car door. Gayle gets in the backseat and for some reason the driver rolls his eyes and slams the door behind her. Reg takes note of the company name, the taxi's plate, and the car number.

"Do you know these two men who are standing outside smoking?"

"No, I don't, but I'll ask the bouncers."

"No that's okay, we'll do that ourselves. Now, as for the other staff, the dancers, can you give us the name and contact info for whoever was closest with Gayle? We want to learn more about her and–"

"Sad to say, Detective, but there's no one. Gayle didn't make friends with any of the girls. Unfortunately the opposite is true, I was constantly getting complaints about Gayle. I guess she started a lot of fights and was accused of having sticky fingers."

"Did anyone file charges?"

"Oh no, the girls are too smart to leave anything of real value lying around. No, it was just petty thefts, pilfering."

Grant digests this news of a flaw in Gayle's character causing animosity among her coworkers. They'd already heard about her stealing money from her young sister, and borrowing her brother's car without permission. Plus there was that cheque of her mother's found in her pocket.

"Reg, have you got all the info you need?" he asks. At his partner's nod he turns to Sol Stein and thanks him for his assistance. "We'll be back in the office on Monday and will be waiting for the rest of the video."

Sol escorts them to the door and stays to listen when they question the two husky men manning the entrance. They claim not to have recognized either of the smokers and got the impression, from what they overheard, that those men didn't know each other. They simply shared the camaraderie of their vice. Both bouncers confirmed that neither of the men came to the Club tonight.

Grant and Reg each have their own vehicles so they part company in the parking lot with Reg saying he'll call the night dispatch at the cab company now to see if he can get the ball rolling right away.

They say good night and while driving home Grant reminds himself of all the broken Covid rules so he can pass the information on to his boss. He hopes she might get the Club's liquor licence pulled, or even shut down, for a few days. *People need to respect the regulations*, he thinks. *Paying fines isn't good enough, especially with how much money compliant businesses are losing.*

He's staying at his own place tonight, not wanting to disturb Judith since he didn't know how late he'd be. He's just pulled into the driveway of his apartment when his phone beeps with a text. It's a message from Reg telling him that the cab driver booked off for the long weekend but is expected back for a 12-hour shift on Monday. The delay is a minor annoyance but after all there's really no rush, so Grant just shrugs it off.

Easter Sunday Dinner

Judith is watching Lila, marvelling at how calmly she moves about the kitchen. Stirring a sauce, pulling out the roasting pan to poke a fork in the potatoes, adding butter to vegetables in the steamer, all without fuss or hurry.

When the oven door was open an enticing, fragrant aroma filled the room and Judith inhales deeply, her taste buds primed. She and Grant have arrived for Easter dinner which Lila is cooking at the Penner residence.

"When you told me Beth had invited a friend to dinner I just assumed it was Dusty but now you're telling me it's another boy? What happened with those two?"

Shaking her head with a smile Lila says: "Remember how worried I was about Beth getting her heart broken? Well, I worried for nothing because I think Beth is the heart-breaker. She liked Dusty a lot, but he's been gone for months now and she isn't bothered in the least.

This new fellow is called... oh heck, I forget. She did tell me, let me think...ummm, nope, nothing. I mean I know it's one of the a-r-y names like Larry, Gary, Terry—"

"Terry is spelled with an e," interrupts Judith.

"Well yes, I know that, sheesh you're so nitpicking! I just meant how it sounds. Barry, Cary, Gary, Harry, Harry! that's it. He's called Harry."

"I'm precise, not nitpicking. Anyways, how did she meet this Harry? Do you know?"

"Mm-hmm, they met through his sister. She goes to our school."

Before Judith can ask for further details Beth comes in and shyly asks Lila if it would be okay to use her mother's *special occasion* china for tonight's dinner. Judith tactfully retreats to check up on the men. Smiling at the girl's hopeful expression Lila declares that *real china will be perfect for our Easter dinner!*

"This way even if the food isn't up to par at least it will be nicely presented. That's so important according to those cooking shows we watch."

"Oh Lila, we both know any meal you cook will be exceptional even if it's served on paper plates!" replies Beth with a giggle.

She fetches the step-stool and climbs up to open one of the top kitchen cupboards. "There's enough for eight people, place-settings they call them, and there are serving bowls and a platter and a gravy... thingy–"

"Boat," Lila says with a smile, continuing: "It's called a gravy boat and I have no idea why."

"Maybe the shape?"

"Judith!" calls Lila into the living room, "Why do they call a gravy boat a boat?"

Returning to the kitchen Judith looks from Lila to Beth and shrugs her shoulders saying: "Why on earth do you think I'd know? I don't even own a set of china dishes."

"Well since you're getting married you probably will soon."

"Really? Hmm, do I get to pick? Oh I like these. It's called a pattern, right?" Picking up a plate she turns it over and reads out *Greenwich, Minton.* "I like this, it's not fussy and of course green is my favourite colour."

"This is an old set of dishes," explains Beth proudly. "They were my great-grandmother's, and she passed them on to my grandmother, then my mother got them, and now, well I guess they're mine."

"Then we better be very careful of them. Go ahead and hand them down to us just a few at a time. We'll give the top ones a quick wash or maybe just a dusting will do? and then we can get the table set," instructs Lila.

After passing down all the chinaware Beth folds up the stool and turns to Judith saying: "You haven't mentioned Panda, any new photos?"

"I thought you'd never ask! Hard to believe but some people find it boring when I produce the latest two hundred photos of my adorable, photogenic kitten," replies Judith with a grin.

"That's me!" says Beth raising her hand to point to herself. "I'm one of those people."

Judith and Beth roll their eyes at each other. Judith picks up her phone and quickly scrolls to the Photo Gallery then passes it over for Beth to pay homage to the antics of the winsome cat.

"Oh she's so adorable! and she's really grown since I saw her. How old is she now?"

"She's coming up to six months. Next week I take her in to be spayed."

"Aww, poor baby. Will they keep her overnight?"

"No, it's day surgery and they've given me care instructions for when she comes home. Very straightforward and nothing to be alarmed about. At least, that's what they say."

"Surgery sound expensive," comments Lila from whatever task she's busy with at the stove.

"It's all paid for, or rather when Grant bought Panda from the store the price included the spay or neuter, depending on male or female. That's the great thing about buying a rescue. And it means I already know what vet she's going to. Prepaying encourages people to get it done which is important if you're not planning to breed the animal."

Unconsciously rubbing her still-small baby bump Lila asks: "Aren't you supposed to let them have a litter first? I'm sure I heard something about that."

In a clipped voice Judith states: "No. It's cruel. Just like letting them outside is cruel. It sounds good, you know letting the cat run free, but it's way too dangerous. Predators, cars, serial-killers-in-the-making.."

Beth laughs at the exaggeration before telling the women that at school another student's environmental project for science class was about how outdoor cats have decimated bird populations and even threatened some species with extinction.

"I expect she's someone who owns a bird," sniffs Judith.

Lila chimes in saying: "I've never really considered birds to be pets. Same with fish, I mean they're nice, pretty to look at, and they need to be looked after, but you can't cuddle them or anything." She opens the oven door to remove the roasting pan and again the tantalizing aroma of seasoned meat wafts out.

"Dinner smells delicious, Lila, what is it?"

"We're having roasted leg of lamb so I hope you weren't expecting a turkey-and-stuffing dinner."

"No, I didn't even think about what you'd be cooking. I know it's always good. I've never had lamb, though."

"Well, we've also got a baked ham in case anyone doesn't like lamb. It's not really an acquired taste but it does have a unique flavour. You know, lots of people who say they don't like lamb have only ever eaten mutton which is completely different."

"Beth, I'm looking forward to meeting this new guy, Dusty's replacement?"

Beth laughs at Judith's remark. "Dusty and I are still friends but he's moved to Toronto. You remember how things weren't great between him and his Dad? Well, his parents are having a trial separation and now he's moved with his mother to her sister's place back East.

We text and stuff but he's meeting new people and well, me too. As for Harry I'm afraid he can't come after all."

"Yes, I was going to tell you Judith. Unfortunately Harry's older sister has just died. A sudden death and it's been a real shock to the whole family."

"Oh, a car accident?"

"No, it was a drug overdose."

"Another one? It's becoming an epidemic. So sad, and it always seems worse when someone dies around a holiday because each year is another reminder."

Grant and Brian have come into the kitchen to fetch cold beers from the fridge. Overhearing Judith's comment Grant states:

"When someone was deeply loved they're still with you every day, you don't need a special reminder, but you're right about holidays being tough. Although in the case of my mother there are so many happy memories of good times, silly times, festive holiday dinners, that it's a happy-sad thing, if that makes sense."

The room is getting crowded now and Lila shoos them out saying: "Beth and I've got this handled, so go back to sitting in the living-room till we call you to the table."

Judith links her arm with Grant's and dramatically whispers: "C'mon, don't make the cook mad or we'll get kicked outta here and I want to eat."

"It does smell awfully good," Grant stage-whispers back.

Putting on a mock-stern expression Lila says: "Grant you can tell Brian all about your latest case, which I'm sure won't be appropriate for our holiday dinner conversation."

"Matter of fact we don't have any mysteries at the moment, touch wood." He adds, leaning over to rap on the cutting board.

"Oh Grant, don't be superstitious!" cries Judith, "And don't tempt fate!"

"Who's superstitious now?" he laughs.

"They say it's bad luck to be superstitious." quips Brian.

Fifteen minutes later the five of them have just seated themselves round the table when the doorbell rings. They look at one another in surprise until Beth's phone dings from it's charging station – she's not allowed to bring it to the table when they're eating – and she scrambles from her chair exclaiming: "That must be Harry!"

The four adults unashamedly interrupt their conversation to eavesdrop. They hear the happiness in Beth's voice when she says *oh good, you made it*. A male voice replies hesitantly, too low to hear, but Beth's is confident as she orders him to *come in, come in*.

Brian pulls another chair up to the table and Lila fetches a sixth place-setting. When the two teenagers enter the dining-room Harry is introduced all around and Grant is taken aback to discover they've met before. Grant and Reg called at Harry's home with the unhappy news about Gayle Boudreau's death.

He can see that Harry recognizes him as well, but nothing is said about his sister so Grant figures *why bring it up and ruin this festive occasion?*

He's a well-built young man but sitting flanked by Grant and Brian he looks boyish. He and Beth are obviously very interested in each other.

Soon the youth is digging into the food heaped on his plate while keeping his eyes fixed on Beth, and nodding along to her conversation.

Grant helps himself to the garlic-roasted vegetables but before passing on the dish he admires the china and asks Judith if she's picked out her pattern yet.

"Pattern? I don't sew... oh you mean dishes?"

"That's right, we were just talking about patterns and I said you'd probably get china for a wedding present," Lila reminds her.

"Not just china," says Grant, "but crystal and silverware, too. You need to go out and make your selections then get registered."

At his fiancée's blank look he explains: "Registered for wedding and shower gifts. You want to make it as easy as possible for people so get listed on several gift registries. Birks is good, and there's Bowrings, and The Bay, of course," he concludes.

Beth points out: "All the posh shops start with a B."

"All the best people, too," murmurs Harry but Lila hears him and says: "That's right, Harry. Isn't it Brian?" emphasizing the B.

Still thinking of store registries Grant exclaims: "Oh and Amazon makes it really convenient since they deliver, so definitely register there."

In the silence that follows everyone notices that Judith is annoyed with Grant, but no one is sure why until she says angrily: "I am NOT going to BEG for presents, Grant, and I don't want you to either."

"Judith! that's not how people see Gift Registries," exclaims Lila.

Brian puts in: "Even I've heard about them and how it's way easier for people to shop that way."

"That's right, everyone expects it nowadays. And the stores keep track of what's been bought so you don't get two or three of the same thing. Judith, it's perfectly normal."

"Grant you and I have each lived on our own for years so we've already got two of pretty much everything from vacuums to air-fryers. We don't need gifts and honestly what would I do with a full set of china? I don't entertain and I really don't want to start but if I did my everyday dishes are perfectly fine. Besides, I like my Danbyware and I thought you did, too."

"I do, I like all your stuff because you have great taste but... wow I never thought for a minute that this would be a problem. Wedding gifts, I mean. Um, you're right we don't need stuff but I don't want people to give us money."

"Well of course not!" Judith exclaims.

"But Judith, guests want to give something."

"That's right, it's partly a sense of obligation for the meal but mostly out of affection for the couple," states Lila.

Judith looks between her friends and biting back any retort says: "Well let's talk about something else right now, okay?"

Reaching over to squeeze her hand Grant's voice is gentle when he says: "Sure thing. We'll work it out."

Harry gets up to leave as soon as the meal is over and declines Lila's offer of some leftovers to take home explaining lots of neighbours have been dropping off casseroles and stuff.

He surprises everyone when he speaks directly to Judith saying: "One of the neighbours mentioned that plenty of families name a charity for donations instead of people sending flowers and maybe you can have something like that if you don't want wedding presents."

Everyone just stares and he blushes, mumbling: "Or not, forget I said anything."

"No! Harry that's brilliant! It's a wonderful idea, isn't it Grant?"

Smiling Grant agrees that it sounds like a perfect solution. Still blushing, but grinning now, Harry says his goodbyes and thanks Lila and Brian for the meal. He politely nods to Judith and Grant.

He's made a good impression on all of the adults and they look on indulgently when Beth walks him to the door where they whisper together for a few minutes.

Having scraped his dessert plate clean Brian now sits staring at it with a bemused expression on his face. Beth returns to the table and giggles: "Dad! What's with that goofy grin?"

Brian smiles widely as he tells his daughter: "These dishes sure bring back memories. I have an image in my mind of you at, oh probably six or seven since your two front teeth are missing, sitting right there with a big red Christmas bow in your hair. And Mandy wore a matching one,

I think she made them, and the two of you looked so pretty, you made such a perfect picture."

Beth darts around the table to give her father a hug. The two share a happy moment remembering. It's a touching scene that warms Judith's heart until she catches sight of Lila with a tremulous smile frozen on her face. Judith wonders if there are many instances like this one that leave her friend feeling shut out. Looking back at the Penner pair she's reassured to see how they both smile fondly at Lila.

Beth starts gathering up dishes and both Judith and Grant help. They wave off their hosts' protests insisting Lila and Brian should relax. Brian leaves his chair to move into the one Beth vacated. Glancing over her shoulder as she enters the kitchen Judith sees Brian slip his arm around Lila's shoulders and give her a kiss. She's happy to see Lila snuggle closer.

***

Judith also noticed the earlier silent exchange Harry had with Grant, and quizzes him about it on the drive home. Grant rubs his hand over his chin and thinks a moment before replying.

"On Saturday Reg and I delivered a notification of death to a family who live out at the trailer park. When the death is due to a medical incident or a traffic accident that's normally handled by uniform, but when it looks like drugs are involved we get called in.

Giving a death notification to the next-of-kin is probably the worst aspect of this job. The news is usually heartbreaking and when it isn't... which was kinda the case with the Boudreau family, well, then it's chilling."

Grant had a beer and some wine at dinner so Judith is doing the driving. Since she's cautious and never takes her hands off the wheel she doesn't reach out to him but does murmur sympathetically.

He continues: "This family was shocked rather than teary. We got the impression that the daughter, Gayle, had such a strong, domineering personality that the family couldn't imagine anything happening to her. They showed more disbelief than distress.

Oh! the victim's sister is one of your students, a pretty adolescent called Didi but I don't remember her last name. The victim and her mother are called Boudreau, but the younger brother, Harry, and the sister each have different surnames."

"A pretty student called Didi must be Didi Jackson. Didi really is her name you know, it's not short for Deana or Deirdre, it's not a nickname. Her given name is Didi. Oh this is sad news. She's a well-behaved pupil with good grades so I don't know her."

"Sorry, what?"

With a light laugh Judith explains: "I really don't have much to do with the good girls, most of the ones I meet with are the troublemakers."

"The dreaded trip to the Principal's Office, eh?"

Primly Judith replies: "I certainly hope so! but what on earth was her sister doing taking drugs at night at our school? She looked way older than Didi, too."

"She is. Reg has all the pertinent facts but I think there's like a sixteen or seventeen year gap between the oldest and youngest siblings in the family."

"Oh Grant! Do you think Didi is really Gayle's daughter?"

"Umm no... and what kind of books are you reading?"

"I read the Classics, as you very well know. And maybe the odd book of *mommy porn* that somebody's left lying around."

Grant snorts a laugh at her admission. Returning to his previous comment he explains: "We get involved when it's a case of suspected drug overdose in the hopes the family can point us to the supplier. Very often they don't even know about the drug use but sometimes they'll accuse one of the victim's friends or point the finger at someone in the neighbourhood. You remember that trouble with the squatters dealing drugs out at the trailer park and causing the big fire?"

Judith shudders at the memory exclaiming: "People actually died in that fire, and some of the firefighters were badly burned too, right?"

Solemnly Grant confirms: "Yes, four residents died, and two firefighters were hospitalized with serious injuries. The explosion of ether gas made it a very dangerous, hot-burning fire.

The remnants of a household fire are sickening. I mean, seeing such things as a clock melted into the wall, an oven door blown off, everyday items reshaped into unidentifiable plastic blobs is gut-wrenching... and of course that horrible, synthetic smell."

"Don't think about it, Grant. Hopefully you'll never have to visit another scene like that."

Resting his hand on her thigh Grant gives Judith a squeeze and in a lighter tone says: "What's that expression? from your lips to God's ear. Amen to that thought!"

"Do you believe in God?"

"This conversation is wandering down some strange by-roads... I was talking about neighbours noticing more than you think. Oh! are you asking because it's Easter?"

"No, I never thought of that. I'm just curious. I don't, if you're wondering."

"Well... I believe in something but I can't define it so let's just leave it at that. You've already agreed to a church wedding so I guess you must be doing that for my sake, hmm?"

"Well you spoke about getting married in a church and honestly it doesn't matter one way or the other to me so I'm happy to go along with your plans. Now you're the one sidetracking me, Grant. We were talking about that woman's death from drugs. I know you said last night's visit to see strippers–"

"Not to see them, but to interview them. I already explained that, didn't I?"

"Mmm, well... it was part of this investigation?"

"Yes, but we didn't learn much. We didn't even get a chance to interview the dancers," Judith rolls her eyes at him, "because it was time to shut down for the night. Not that they had the slightest intention of doing so until we showed up.

Anyhow, surveillance video showed that Gayle Boudreau got into a cab and we've called the company who will have the driver get in touch with us. Her time is unaccounted for after she left work, which the camera showed was just before 10:15, and we suspect she's the one who made the anonymous phone call at 11:30. We don't know where she was, or who she was with, but we expect to get an address when we get hold of the cabbie. Dispatch didn't have one and no call was logged because she picked up the taxi outside of the club."

They arrive at Judith's apartment because Grant is staying the night. He's pretty much moved in full-time. They had to cancel their proposed house-hunting trip yesterday but they're both keen to find a home and make a move soon. Prices are exorbitant, but after years of professional work they've each built up decent-sized nest-eggs for a downpayment.

***

In the privacy of Brian's bedroom he and Lila also discuss Harry Drapeau.

"He's a different type of boy from Dusty, much quieter," she comments.

"I like him, well what I know of him. He didn't stay long, understandable in the circumstances, and you're right he didn't have much to say."

"I wonder if he's usually that way? or if he's subdued because of his sister dying. At his age I'd guess this is probably the first death of someone close. Beth takes it all in her stride though, doesn't she? She's got such a comfortable and calm way about her."

"Yeah, she takes after her mother. Mandy was the same way, always cool and unruffled. Nothing ever fazed her," he states with a smile of remembrance.

Lila doesn't respond to Brian's words but does add: "I don't think any boy is ever going to break Beth's heart."

Walking over to take Lila in his arms Brian gives her a kiss then drops to his knees and kisses her slightly extended belly, too. He tilts back his head to read Lila's expression when he says: "I think I've been patient long enough, sweetheart. It's time to set the date for our wedding."

Easter Monday Holiday

Sol is embarrassed at how little money was collected in the whip-round to buy a wreath for Gayle Boudreau's coffin. He hadn't realized just how much the dancer was disliked, even hated, despite all the years she worked at Heavenly Bodies.

He'd told the police that no one was close to her and that's true. Thinking back he can't name a single girl who would call Gayle her friend. He wonders how many - if any - will bother to attend her funeral.

Today he's taking Gayle's belongings back to her family although he doesn't know if her parents will be home this Easter Monday. He knows she was living back at home but as to why – maybe a divorce? -he has no idea.

Most people are back at work since Good Friday is the statutory holiday. *Nevertheless it's a pleasant drive and it's not like I have anything else to do on a Christian holiday*, he smiles to himself.

Glancing at the dashboard clock he worries that it might be a little early to drop in on someone. He can't phone, he doesn't have the number, and only has the address because he had to send a ride-share for Gayle on Friday night.

Sol doesn't sleep more than four or five hours a night. His routine is to close up the Club by locking the doors, putting the receipts and cash in the safe, and making sure all the electricals are off. Then, after having a short sleep, he's back in the morning to let the cleaners in.

While they do their thing he checks stock, orders inventory, and deals with staff issues. There's always something, some problem or issue, when you've got a dozen women and half-a-dozen men working together.

Today his work began in the dancers' dressing room. The staff lockers at the club aren't big and don't hold much, but even so the contents of Gayle's are pathetically meager.

Sol packed a thin cardigan badly in need of a wash; a pair of sky-high heels, one with a broken ankle strap; a jumble of receipts, envelopes, and old lottery tickets; and messy bottles and tubes of make-up. There isn't enough to fill a plastic grocery bag. *Now that the brick of coke is gone that is,* he grumbles sourly.

The gang won't fire him over the police raid, but the entire cost of the confiscated drug will come out of his share of the club's profits. It'll take a few months to re-pay that loss which means he'll be out-of-pocket for awhile.

If the police keep coming around chasing away our customers it's gonna take more than a few months to make up that money, he thinks. *And obviously I'm gonna have to make up the difference in the cost of a funeral wreath, too.*

Arriving at the Edgemont Trailer Park Sol finds the right unit and knocks at the door. Harry answers so Sol hands the boy the bag and asks to see his mother. When Harry turns to holler: "Mom! Door!" a curious Didi comes down the hall and Sol's eyes widen at the young beauty. Harry elbows his sister to nudge her back down the hallway saying *He wants to see Mom, not you.*

Cherysh comes from the room on the right, the kitchen, and listens impassively to Sol's speech of condolence. Sol hands over an envelope of cash explaining it's Gayle's final wage packet and tips. Cherysh immediately opens it and counts the bills. She extracts one and folds it into her palm without comment.

Sol feels awkward, uncertain what to say, when confronted with the dead woman's dry-eyed mother. A considerably younger mother than he had imagined.

"Any date yet for the funeral I'm sure some—?" he begins asking but Cherysh cuts him off saying the police haven't released the body and "I can't afford to do much of anything anyhow."

Thinking for a moment Sol reaches back into his pocket and taking out a second envelope explains: "This money was contributed by Gayle's co-workers to buy a wreath but perhaps...?"

Cherysh takes it and grudgingly says *thank everyone for us*. She doesn't say anything else and Sol wonders if she's waiting for another envelope to appear, as if he were a magician producing endless envelopes from pockets. Cherysh is inching the door closed so Sol takes the hint and tells her goodbye.

Settling back in his car he thinks *that stunning girl will probably end up having a life just like Gayle's and that will be a real shame.* Then, mulling it over, he decides *no, this one has a protective brother to watch over her. Gayle never had anyone in her corner.* Sadly he shakes his head musing *not even her mother.*

Harry has been hovering in the hall and now hands his mother the plastic bag of belongings taken from Gayle's locker at work. She carries it into the kitchen and dumps the contents on the table.

The shoes clatter to the floor and a lipstick rolls off the edge to join them. After shuffling through the items Cherysh shoves everything back in the bag except for a stack of papers. It looks like trash, just some receipts and bills, but she wants to check everything out.

Near the top of the pile is a letter written in purple pen, an affectation of Gayle's that Cherysh recognizes. As she glances through it her face pales and she exhales a *huh!*

"What is it? What's wrong?" asks Harry, concerned by the look on his mother's face.

She hands him the letter saying "It's your sister's suicide note."

Harry is dumbfounded but before he can utter a word his mother continues: "Except it's not. It's a forgery that's been planted with her stuff."

"Are you sure?"

"Read it for yourself," she begins and then nods when her son says *Oh!*

"Mom, what are you going to do?" Harry asks just as Didi sidles into the kitchen plaintively asking: "What's going on?"

"I'm going to have to call those police back and give it to them. It's their problem now."

She thrusts her hand out to her daughter passing on the folded twenty dollar bill and saying: "Here, put it back in your piggy bank."

***

Neither Grant nor Reg have much to say on the drive over to Cherysh Boudreau's home. Both are perplexed at her news that included with Gayle's belongings from the strip club is a suicide note.

Each man is puzzling out the idea that Gayle wrote the note and put it in her locker then left the club early, phoned in the tip to the drug squad, and hours later overdosed herself. Why wouldn't she have the note with her? Why leave it with the drugs?

"To make sure it was found and didn't get tossed away in a cover-up?" suggests Reg.

"Could be... but what if it was to implicate the owner of the drugs? Gayle's little bit of revenge."

"Then she'd have to know she was going to die that night. I mean, she phones in the tip knowing the drug squad will execute a search and find the cocaine. What else will they find? Her suicide note. Maybe she figured leaving the note would buy her some time? because means now they're looking for a body, a victim, instead of a criminal in possession."

"Except they weren't. Remember? Tom Collins was just about to put out an APB on Gayle so they weren't searching for a body which means they didn't find the note."

"So you think it got planted after the raid? But who had access? I'm sure customers can't go in the dressing-room, and maybe not the bouncers, either."

"Or the police just left it in place. Their warrant was only for drugs, nothing else, not even papers."

"Ugh, you're right. Time to stop guessing, forget I said anything."

"It's possible she somehow planned to use it when everything caught up with her. Maybe claiming she was severely depressed or something? I guess we'll never know."

Arriving at the trailer Cherysh opens the door and directs the two men to the kitchen. The note, written in purple ink, is the only thing on the table. Both men lean in to read without touching it.

"Does this look like your daughter's handwriting?" asks Grant.

"It doesn't even look like her name," retorts Cherysh. The detectives turn surprised faces back to the note and spot the signature, now understanding exactly what Cherysh means.

She confirms that saying: "It's never been Gail-with-an-i, always Gayle-with-a-y. I should know, I'm the one who named her."

"See? The note spells her name wrong!" Harry points out.

"Whoever signed this so-called suicide note it sure wasn't my daughter."

***

Mornings come far too soon, thinks Lila. She's slept over at Brian's place but he's already up and his side of the bed is cool. It was late by time they'd cleaned up the kitchen and put away the leftovers last night.

Then we argued over setting a wedding date, she thinks feeling guilty. *And I haven't been sleeping well lately.*

Lila wakens a couple of times during the night and it takes her a good twenty minutes to fall back asleep. She can't seem to shut off the thoughts swirling in her restless mind. Despite knowing that jittery nerves aren't good for the baby. She can't help it, there's no escaping this reaction to all the pressure she's feeling.

Brian is pushing her to set a date and her mother keeps calling to remind her they're going to have to make their travel arrangements soon. Summer is a busy time for the airlines and they want to be sure of getting a booking.

At least I don't have to worry about getting Mom and Dad into a hotel since Mrs. Piernitsky has very kindly offered the use of one of her spare bedrooms. Since there are no hotels in Edgemont we'd have to be driving back and forth to Calgary otherwise.

Reluctantly climbing out of her warm bed she wonders why it's so easy to sleep in in the morning, but so hard to fall asleep in the night. *I'm too tired for mysteries,* she grumbles to herself as she heads for the bathroom.

There's a chance Lila's wedding will occur during the Stampede which means no vacancies at hotels, motels, or B and Bs. Even the campgrounds within driving distance will all be fully booked. *Why am I worrying about campgrounds?* Lila thinks, wondering why she's fretting over all the wrong things.

She and Brian decided on a Justice of the Peace at Calgary City Hall and then discovered that's not a thing. Not outside of the movies that is, or at least not in Alberta. Here they need a Marriage Commissioner to officiate at their wedding, and first that person needs their marriage licence in order to perform the civil ceremony.

Brian is a doer. Once he and Lila set a date he'll take care of hiring the Marriage Commissioner and he'll book the venue. They've already asked Judith and Grant to stand up with them so those two will fulfill the roles of witnesses.

Interestingly the place they choose for the ceremony can be anywhere and Brian's decided a restaurant will work out best.

He can't get the marriage licence on his own. Both he and Lila need to go to the Registry Office together to show their identification and sign their names. They meet all the legal requirements and don't need to provide copies of their spouses death certificates which surprises Lila. The licence will cost $40, plus the Registry Agent's fee, and is valid for three months.

That still leaves a lot for Lila to do. She needs to buy a dress, choose her flowers, and make her guest list. She told Brian she wants an Italian restaurant where they can get a set meal that will ensure all the guests are well-fed. He's already told her he's footing the bill and frowned in refusal when she offered to pay half. *Save your money to buy cute baby stuff,* he said.

Lila knows she doesn't have the luxury of time. She needs to pick a date so people can get started making all the necessary arrangements. She's leaning towards the end of May. The weather should be nice, while travel and bookings should be easy since the tourist season doesn't really get going until school's out at the end of June.

She hasn't mentioned this to anyone yet, knowing that once she does the whole process will begin and she'll get swept along despite any concerns she has.

Her brain knows there is no reason to hesitate but in her heart of hearts she's uncertain. She knows she and Brian will definitely marry, and before their child is born too, but... something is holding her back from taking that final step of commitment.

I sure wish I still had Rev Robbie to talk to. He'd sort me out in no time, she thinks with a teary smile, remembering the no-nonsense personality of the now-deceased cleric she'd grown so close to.

Why Fake a Suicide?

George Grant leans back in his chair deep in thought while staring out the window of the office he shares with Reg. The sky is overcast and looks full of snow although there's no precipitation in the forecast. Each morning the windshield of his car is frosted over but at least he can clear it with the defogger, no more scraping off ice.

Fingers crossed, he thinks his face frowning at the knowledge they're still in the grip of winter weather even though the calendar says it's spring. Daytime highs are good, but he spotted a couple of rabbits in the parking-lot and their coats were still solid white. He figures there's one more dump of snow to come.

"So what's got you bothered about this new case?" asks Reg seeing the expression on Grant's face.

"Actually I was grumbling to myself about the weather–"

"Why? It's great here," interrupts Reg. "I was watching the weather report for back home and they've got rain, freezing rain, freezing fog, and snow every day. Right across the whole Maritimes. 'Course they don't believe me when I say it's dry and above zero here."

"Oh yeah this winter's been okay, except for those few really cold days and they didn't last. Truth is I'm using the weather as a distraction.

Discovering this so-called accidental overdose might actually be a murder is getting to me. So far we've only done the next-of-kin notification and spoken to the victim's boss. And that was just to get a lead on the drug trail, not a real interview. Now Cherysh Boudreau calls us about this phony note. I'm frustrated that we've wasted so much time."

"Can't really blame the first responders for thinking it was simply misadventure, though. I mean, it's heartbreaking how common fentanyl overdoses have become. I've read the statistics and more than two people, usually in their early thirties, die every day. Every single day.

That's way, way too young to lose your life – especially 'cause you want to get high."

"Or get out of pain."

"True that. I heard somebody say the trouble with the drug is that it does its job too well. That's why the hospitals don't want Canada to stop importing it but I don't know... it's just so deadly."

"Yes I know you're right, Reg. The way that it was handled makes sense. But now that this ridiculous suicide note has turned up – they didn't even spell Gayle's name right! First off, no one even thought it was suicide until the note was found, and then why pretend it's suicide when it's already been ruled as misadventure? Isn't a verdict of accidental death by overdose the best possible result? Suicide isn't preferable to that, right?"

"No, I mean if it was the other way round then sure, people would prefer accident to suicide, but I don't see that in this case. I mean it's not like there's a concern about not being allowed a church burial or anything. If that even applies anymore? I have no idea. As it stands her mother wasn't even happy about claiming the body, was she? And there's no insurance policy or death benefit coming–"

"Don't even go there," Grant interrupts. "We've got enough suspects! Either the killer didn't think they'd get an accidental death verdict and planted the note as cover, or–"

"Or somebody created that obviously fake suicide note to open up a murder investigation."

"And from what we're learning about Gail Boudreau well, I don't like to victim-blame but in her case homicide is definitely an option."

"You mean gang-related because of the stolen cocaine?"

"Possibly, but I suspect we'll find plenty of drama on the domestic front as well. It felt like there was some problem between her and her mother, and I suspect Mom's boyfriend was involved in that. I know we only had a preliminary interview with them but didn't you think the tension in the room was off the charts?"

"The two siblings were shocked at their sister's death, but not saddened, and though they're young they're old enough to kill. It must have been awkward with you having met the boy before in a social setting–"

"You have no idea. He joined us at the Penner's for Easter dinner and at first Beth, Brian's daughter, said her boyfriend wasn't coming because his sister had just died but I never made the connection. Well, why would I?"

"Yeah, we barely spoke to the kids when we originally made the notification. Edgemont is a small community so that sort of thing is bound to happen now and then, though."

"I guess. If I think there's a conflict or any kind of problem I'll take it to the Chief and let her decide."

Reg just nods before picking up the earlier train of thought. "The badly faked note is an amateur move, but there's no way her own brother and sister wouldn't know how she spells her name."

"And even if the wrong spelling was done on purpose to misdirect us they'd have left the note in the trailer. There's no way they could plant that note. They couldn't even get inside the club never mind getting into her locker. And the biker gang that owns the strip club sure isn't amateur."

"Tell me about them."

"Well," Grant leans back in his chair, staring up towards the ceiling instead of out the window this time. He thinks for a moment before answering: "I know *of* them, but not much *about* them. *The Screaming Devils MC* is Calgary's problem or it was until Gayle Boudreau died in Edgemont.

I've liaised with the local cops who said this motorcycle gang has never officially come to their attention. They don't have a clubhouse in Calgary. They own the Heavenly Bodies strip joint but leave it in the hands of the manager we met, Solomon Stein. From what the sergeant said the gang has several venues throughout the province and they run them all the same way.

They hire strippers locally but also bring in girls that get moved from one location to the other. I'm waiting to hear back from the RCMP to see if they can tell us where the club is based out of, and what they know about them."

"Sounds like it could be sex trafficking."

"I think so too, and I hope to God we're wrong."

Reg thinks a moment looking puzzled. Finally he says: "So her calling the cops to raid the place for cocaine sure was a dangerous move. And the report said it was stashed in her locker, right? that's just suicidal behaviour." Grim-faced he adds: "No pun intended."

"Yeah, and the other girls working there complained to the manager about Gayle. Seems like she caused trouble wherever she went, and she's still causing it."

"No, this trouble is being caused by whoever wants us to find out the truth. They don't want it to stay buried with Gayle."

Grant sits up saying: "I told that manager, Sol... Sol Stein, that I wanted the surveillance tapes from inside the Club today but I haven't heard anything. I'll give him a call. And what do we know his movements?"

Flipping through his notebook Reg finds the appropriate spot and reads the result. "Stein has a candyapple-red 2002 Ford Thunderbird convertible and he parks it right under one of the cameras in their lot. I had a look and it's a beauty." Grant smiles at his partner knowing Reg is an enthusiast, his personal car is a 1970 Chevelle.

Happily launching into an explanation Reg continues: "Ford re-issued an updated version of its T-Bird model from the fifties. Did you ever see that movie *American Graffiti?* Well this is the same car, the one with the porthole window, that Suzanne Somers drove. Except her car was white in the movie.

Stein's car never moved from the time he arrived until after the Drug Squad left. Their arrival basically shut the place down and he stayed with them the whole time. Now it's still possible he left for awhile: he could have borrowed someone else's car, or got a ride, or something. But it's going to be hard to pin down reliable witnesses. The interior tapes will help us there."

"You're right. If he keeps dragging his feet about releasing them I'll mention that," chuckles Grant picking up the phone.

***

Parking in the school lot Judith is annoyed to see that the police haven't been by to remove their yellow tape yet. Still sitting in her car she calls the police station right away. This isn't something she needs to

86

bother Grant with but she has no compunction about using his name is necessary.

When the Desk Sergeant answers she explains who she is and demands that the police come by to clear away their tape. The man explains *we need clearance from the Medical Examiner's office first* but knowing of Judith's engagement to his boss courteously adds *I'll phone them now.*

"Thank you. It's vital this is all cleared away before the students show up tomorrow morning."

"We'll do our best, ma'am."

Judith has to accept that. She comforts herself with the knowledge that their elderly caretaker will be by hours before the girls show up and if the tape is still there Mr. Glover won't hesitate to tear it down.

Unlocking the front door Judith walks through the halls of the school with her eyes noticing everything. As Principal Taylor her responsibilities extend to checking that the floors are cleanly scrubbed with no dirty watermarks left on the baseboards to ensuring no errant students are out of their classrooms whispering into cellphones.

Edgemont School for Girls has a ban on students carrying their mobiles. Any calls from family are expected to go through Mrs. Kanji, the school secretary. Samira is the one who decides if a situation warrants interrupting a class.

The school is closed today for the Easter long weekend but Judith's trip through the corridors has a specific destination. She heard Lila say she was coming in today to take an inventory of her supplies, something that's difficult to get done when the students always find excuses to stop by her office. Lila is very popular with the girls. As school nurse she has her own key to the premises, as does the custodian and the secretary.

Judith is on a mission to discuss a rumour she's heard. Seeing her friend sitting at her desk Judith begins speaking right away:

"Hey! I know you're wanting some quiet time to get caught up on your work but I just heard we can get rid of these masks soon, is that true?"

Lila swivels her chair around and gestures for Judith to have a seat on the couch. "I heard the same thing but unfortunately now it's a no-go. The Government has re-introduced stricter Covid measures again because hospitalizations have skyrocketed. It will be on the news shortly."

"But it was, what... just a month ago that we were being congratulated for having *bent the curve?*"

"Yeah, but after all the family gatherings and church services at Easter they're already experiencing another spike in the number of cases."

"Oh speaking of Easter, thanks again for that wonderful meal. Both Grant and I discovered a new-found love for lamb roast."

"It makes a great stew too, well that's what Irish Stew is. Oh and once the weather warms up we'll barbeque a leg on the rotisserie. It's delicious cooked that way."

"Sign us up for that for sure! Anyhow, I found out from Grant that Beth's date Harry is the brother of Didi Jackson."

"Didi? but surely she's–"

"Half-brother. From what I understand there are three children and each has a different father."

"Oh that explains it. Harry's a nice-looking boy but Didi is going to be a knockout. I had her in for a check-up when she joined the track team. She's a great kid: healthy and strong with an open and friendly disposition."

"Beth is on the track team too."

"Yes, that's how she met Harry, it was at a practise at the running-track. I should have realized the reason he was there would be because a friend or family member goes to the school."

"Let's hope that track meets and team practises and school sports don't get stopped again."

"I don't think the public or private enterprise is going to be quite as willing to accept the rules of lockdowns this time. There's going to be plenty of backlash even about extending the mask mandate."

"Well it is disappointing, although I have to admit that the masks do work since we've avoided an outbreak here in our school." Judith perches on the edge of the sofa crossing her legs at the ankle.

"Yeah, the students have been been good about wearing them and also keeping them on. If we were a mixed school they'd be taking them off half the time in order to flirt with the boys."

"They sure would! and of course being girls they've turned them into fashion statements. Young women really are very competitive, aren't they?"

Laughing, Lila exclaims: "Throughout our lives, actually. It's just a myth that as we grow older we lose our combative or adversarial spirit to become nothing but nurturing beings. I mean sure, there are women who deliberately suppress their natures to appease men but Edgemont students aren't encouraged to think that way.

However that's off-topic. I have to say that even if the government does lift the restriction as a school nurse I will always encourage the students to cover up whenever they're suffering from a cough or cold. Mask-wearing has become socially acceptable despite the controversy.

Unfortunately though, as a health professional I have to wonder about the psychological effect of constantly masking."

"I never thought about that. I just find them annoying when I'm trying to understand some of the girls who mumble at the best of times and become incomprehensible when covered up. Plus, it's uncomfortable. It's always such a relief to rub behind my ears while I'm driving home."

"You mean you're not one of those people who drive wearing a mask even when all alone in the car?" teases Lila. "I notice they always seem to be in the passing lane going under the speed limit, too."

"Oh Lila, you turn into Mr. Hyde once you get behind the steering wheel... I'm sure it's because you drive a sports car."

"I'm a perfectly safe driver," Lila interrupts chuckling, "But you're right I do suffer from road *frustration*. I don't *rage* but I do get awfully fed up with ignorant and arrogant drivers. I mean, I love driving and if everyone would just follow the very simple rules of the road it would always be pleasant."

"I agree. I've always loved driving too. Sometimes though, especially if I'm stuck in Calgary at rush-hour, it can be a real ordeal."

"Oh that reminds me, this morning's forecast said the long-range will be staying well above zero so I need to take my snow tires off. They're new and I don't want to wreck them, they cost a bomb."

"Hmm, but it's still pretty early for us to be thinking winter weather is over."

"See I don't know, I'm new to this. In all my years of winter driving in Toronto I never had snow tires but with the way you Westerners drive, well..."

"Ha! I don't switch over because living in an apartment means I have no place to store my other tires. You're lucky to have Mrs. Piernitsky's garage."

"I'm lucky to have Mrs. Piernitsky period!"

The Ex-Roommate

Just before lunch time on Monday Grant and Reg are at the station on the phone, reviewing their notes, and writing up actions.

Reg has heard back from the cab driver and hanging up the phone he relates the conversation to Grant:

"He called me from the dispatch office as soon as he got to work. He's working a 12 to 12 shift today. He said he drove Gayle to an apartment block in the University District and dropped her off at 22:42 according to his log-book. He's got the name of the street but not the number because she directed him where to go once they got close. I wrote down exactly what he said:

There are several buildings together and they all look the same. That new boxy style coloured in light gray, dark gray, and off-white. Bland and boring."

"I like the editorial comments! He must be a chatty cabbie."

"Oh yeah, he went on to tell me he does this full-time. I gather that's a bit unusual, many just work the job on a temporary basis or only part-time hours. Anyhow, he did talk and talk but I've cut it down in my notes here. It wasn't the first building in the complex but that's all he's sure of. Even if he knew which building it was he'd have no idea what the apartment number is.

So, all we've got it that Gayle was dropped off in a complex with several lookalike buildings somewhere east of Shaganappi Trail, near the Children's Hospital. We can't even be sure if she actually went inside one of them. The cabbie said she was pretty rude to him so he didn't hang around."

"You know you've got a point there, Reg. We've been going on the assumption that Gayle had a specific place in mind but there's nothing to tell us if she ever actually reached her planned destination. She could have changed her mind, or she could have met up with the person outside, or could have been waylaid by someone else... who knows?"

They chew over this idea in silence until the front desk calls through saying they've got a man asking to speak to whomever is in charge of the Gayle Boudreau case.

Looking at the office phone Grant asks: "Whomever? What line?"

"No, he's here. In person."

Grant hurriedly replies *we're on our way* as he puts the phone down. "Reg, we've got a live one. With good grammar, too. Let's go meet him and if he isn't a kook we'll take him into an interview room."

"You know, if this was a cop drama on TV then this guy would be our big break, telling us something that cracks the case. But since it's real life he's probably a time-waster."

Reg is wrong, though. The visitor introduces himself as Eric Littner, explaining that Gayle was living with him in his apartment until very recently when she stole his rent money.

"Mr Littner, yes. We heard about you from Gayle's family," states Reg.

The man looks surprised and murmurs *Really?*

"Please come through to an interview room, Mr. Littner. We appreciate you coming in–"

"It was on the late news. I saw the item about Gayle and saying that police were trying to track her movements on Good Friday night. She showed up at my place–"

Grant interrupts asking if the visitor is willing to have the interview recorded, and can they get some basic details first.

"Yes sure, you can record this. The TV said it was a fentanyl overdose. I'm not asking you to confirm that," he hastily adds. "But I do want to do what I can to help."

Everything about Eric Littner from his clean-cut looks to his earnest disposition to his bland clothing of good quality shows he's a serious, sober, stable man. It's almost impossible to imagine him with a stripper girlfriend which makes Grant wonder if he knew about Gayle's job.

Reg is getting the equipment set up and says: "You've come in on your own volition but we still need to read you your rights to ensure that you know–"

"Detective, I'm a lawyer. Mostly litigation but I do know what's what."

"Oh! We understood you owned a business supplies store, or something like that?"

"Yes, that's an investment of mine, a franchise I own. It's a UPS Store and I have a manager running it."

Reg has turned on the machine and now gives the time and date, says who is present, and begins by asking for basic information.

"Mr. Eric Littner, a lawyer, living at...?"

Eric gives his address and it is indeed on the street the cabbie went to. After the preliminary questions are answered for the record Grant asks the witness to give his statement.

"I never expected to see Gayle, that's Gayle Boudreau, ever again so I was shocked, truly shocked, to find her standing outside my door. Someone must have buzzed her in to the building, or maybe she'd had a spare front-door key made?" he muses. Returning to present company he explains: "I changed the lock on my unit right away but I can't do anything about the lobby door. Anyhow, there she was. She stole from me and not just the rent money. She picked up every little expensive thing she could carry.

I sub-let from a friend who owns the condo and I pay my rent in cash because he's worried that subletting might not be allowed. I've had a look at his building's bylaws and am confident he's acting within the regulations which are shockingly incomplete by the way. They're more concerned about short-stay rentals like Airbnb, that sort of thing and– oh! sorry. You aren't interested in any of that.

Okay, so Gayle stole about $2,300 in cash plus some jewellery, my iPad, a couple of watches," holding out his wrist he explains he only wears his Apple watch these days.

"So because she robbed you you ended things and never expected to see her again, is that correct?"

"Yes. I mean we didn't discuss it or actually break up, she just disappeared. I figured she'd go out of her way to avoid me. She knows I'm a lawyer, and that I could have had her arrested for theft."

"Why didn't you file charges?"

Eric Littner studies his hands for a minute before meeting Grant's gaze. He looks from him to Reg and then back again.

Exhaling loudly he states: "I fell in love with her. I know, I know she's a bartender in a strip club which is pretty unsavoury and then I find out she's a crook and now, apparently, a drug user, but I didn't see the red flags.

I gave her my heart and I was devastated to learn the truth about her feelings for me, or rather her lack of them. It's pretty embarrassing to admit to being fooled, you know."

The simple declaration and the naked pain showing on his face convinces the two policemen that he's telling the truth. Grant noted that Gayle lied to Eric about her job, but not the type of place she worked at.

"Gayle begged me to let her move back in and got pretty desperate in her words and behaviour when she realized I wasn't budging. She made an ugly scene but I was adamant that I wouldn't take her back. You see, she killed the love I felt for her when she betrayed my trust. I no longer respected her and if I let her come back well... if I did that I'd no longer respect myself.

Then she accused me of being with someone else and when I explained, quite honestly that *no, there was no one else, I just didn't want her any more*, she got this stunned... kind of defeated look on her face. I..." he stops, unable to go on until he gets his emotions back in check. After a long moment he continues:

"The way she looked made me feel so, so sorry for her. I couldn't hide the pity I felt but, that's all it was. Just pity and regret. She didn't say another word, just turned around and left."

"What time was this?"

"I've been thinking about that, and worked out that Gayle must have arrived about 10:45 and stayed for a bit less than half an hour, because the 11:00 o'clock news had just come on the TV when she walked away."

"Were you at home all night?"

"No, I was at my niece's *Sweet Sixteen* birthday party." He chuckles adding: "I'm sure she'd have preferred a night out with her friends but since that's not possible with the restrictions she had to settle for a family get-together.

It was fun though, and good to see everyone. My sister's husband is part of a big family so they do their own thing on the holidays, like Easter, and I don't usually see them. Friday evening was a good time."

Reg found out how long Gayle had been living with Mr. Littner and after confirming the times again he turns to Grant, signalling that he has all the information he needs.

"I just have one more question, sir," says Grant. "It's really just to clarify something you mentioned earlier. You confirm that you never saw any evidence of Gayle using drugs or carrying them on her person?"

"That's correct. I had absolutely no indication that she had any connection with drugs. I knew Gayle worked with *exotic dancers*, " he makes air quote gestures as he says the phrase, "but that doesn't automatically mean she was on drugs ,and I have to say I really don't think she was. Gayle... Gayle was, well I can say it now, she was a narcissist and they usually take very good care of themselves. I find the idea of Gayle taking a drug as risky, as dangerous, as fentanyl really hard to believe. But, I guess it must be true. Maybe that was her first time?"

"You're right, it is a very dangerous drug, Mr. Littner," replies Grant, not willing to speculate.

The two detectives walk their visitor back out to the front of the police station and shaking hands all round Eric Littner says a quiet *good bye* and leaves.

The men watch him cross the parking lot and Reg lets out a low whistle when Eric gets into a white Mercedes S65 AMG. "That is a very, very expensive car," he comments.

Grant replies: "Gayle probably thought it was just a boring sedan."

Back in their own office again Reg says: "So we can account for Gayle's whereabouts up to shortly after 11:00 pm on the 2nd. She may have made calls or messaged people but with her phone missing it's unlikely we'll ever find out."

"Officer Collins told us that drug tip was phoned in just before midnight, right?"

Reg consults his notes and says, "No, earlier than that. He said 23:30, ugh I can't be bothered with military time. It was 11:30 that night."

"Hmm. Gayle leaves Littner's place, her plans to move back in with him demolished–"

"And really upset by it, from what he said."

"Yeah, so we've got her dealing with a totally unexpected situation, in a high-rise residential area, where did she go next?

She made the phone call soon after leaving Littner's building. Did she make it walking down the street? or did she go some place? Are there any coffee shops around there, or any businesses at all, that stay open late?"

"I'll drive around there tonight, and check things out from say 11:00 onwards. I'll see if anything's open and if it is I'll enquire. Do we have a photo of Gayle?"

"Yeah, I've got her licence in a digital file. I've got her mug shot too but that might be considered prejudicial."

Reg chuckles and asks Grant to print off the driver's licence photo. Looking at the sheet he comments: "At least the big SUSPENDED stamp doesn't cover her face. I expect any late-opening businesses will have good video surveillance, at least that's what I'm hoping, so I'll look into that as well."

"Call me if you come across anything or anyone I should talk to right away, otherwise I'll see you in the morning. I'm off to meet with the Chief. I'm hoping she'll sic the Crown lawyers onto the Club owners to release those surveillance tapes."

"Sounds like a plan, Boss."

***

Judith's expression is introspective and Grant realizes she hasn't heard a word he's said. They've finished dinner and are cleaning up in the kitchen.

"Ahem," he states loudly, followed by silence. Judith's gaze flies up to meet his eyes. The O her mouth forms along with a rapidly rising blush comically exposes her lack of attention.

"Oh Grant, I wasn't listening, I'm so sorry!" she exclaims.

"And here I've been thinking you were listening intently and hanging on every word." Grant sighs theatrically before smiling. A contrite Judith with colour in her cheeks is a pretty sight. "I'll forgive you if you tell me what's on your mind because it looked like you were really deep in thought."

"No, that's okay, you go on with your story. Mine is nothing, really–"

"Well it must be something, sweetheart. C'mon, tell me what it is."

"That's the problem... I don't know what's going on. I have this... threat? yeah, it feels like a threat hanging over me."

Grant's face takes on a stern, serious look as he demands: "Who's threatening you?"

"Oh now I've gone and made it sound all dramatic and it's not, it's... here, let me tell you what I was told and maybe you can make sense of it."

Still frowning Grant nods at her to go ahead.

"Pat Johnson, you remember her, right?"

"Of course I do. Your predecessor, the past principal of the school. I like her, and her husband Mark as well. Is it their problem?"

"No, see Pat phoned me and..." Judith breaks off to recall the conversation. She relates it as closely as she can:

"I got a phone call and Pat's voice came booming over the line, you know how she talks. Anyways she started off demanding to know *Who the hell is Moira Porter-Wilson? and why does she have the School Board all atwitter?* I'd never heard of the woman and had no idea what was going on.

Pat continued saying *this Moira, I can't be bothered with her double-barrelled name, is a new Board Member who has called an urgent meeting.* But Pat didn't know why, and she doesn't know anything about her.

So I asked *How did you hear about this?* and she said *Jane Branston just called me. She's the most level-headed member on that Board. This Wilson-whatever has got everyone worked up so Jane suggested I give you a heads-up about the problem.*

So I said *thanks, but what problem?* and she doesn't know! it seems no one does, except that the phrase *moral turpitude* came up. Or, as Pat put it, *is being hissed at and that's bad news for any school, but particularly a school for girls.*"

Grant thinks about what Judith has told him and asks: "You really have no idea?"

"None! It's got nothing to do with the drug overdose because the meeting was requested before that happened. Pat flat-out demanded to know *who's been misbehaving?* but I can't think of anyone or anything.

They wouldn't use that phrase if this criticism was directed against one of the students so it's got to be about a teacher or staff member but who? Frankly we're all a pretty tame bunch. Eddie and Tanya, two of the teachers, are engaged to each other, and you know that Noel is practically married. The rest of the teachers are single and Xiao is gay, but that's not a problem–"

"Not in a girls' school," Grant interjects with a grin but Judith just shakes her head, unamused.

Ignoring his interruption she continues: "And of the support staff Cindy, our Librarian, and Lila are both engaged, and Samira is already married. Oh, and there's certainly nothing wrong with our old janitor, Mr. Glover."

"Well Judith as Sherlock Holmes would surmise it must be you, then."

"Me? Grant! What are you talking about?"

"Well you are pretty much living in sin with me," he teases, looking smug.

Judith makes a face at him saying people might wonder but no one actually knows.

"Could a student have made an accusation?" Grant asks before hastily adding: "Not a true one, of course but..."

Judith takes his question seriously explaining that's what she's been worrying about. "I can't think of anyone who would but... remember that anonymous letter about me that was planted in the staff room? It's easy enough to smear someone with a lie. Even Suzanne, your ex-partner, implied some nasty stuff about me to Brian Penner–"

"Oh I think she meant alienation, not inappropriate behaviour–"

"Stop defending the woman, Grant. You know perfectly well she was poisonous," Judith snaps. None of her interactions with Detective Suzanne Mirteau were good.

"You're right, she was awful, I just got used to making excuses for her."

Leaning forward Judith plants a quick kiss on his lips saying: "That's why I love you, you're such a nice man."

Grant returns the kiss but more passionately. After a pleasant interval he pulls back and again teases her by saying: "So I guess we're back to you being the subject of the scandal."

"Hmmm... maybe," Judith pretends to consider the idea.

"So when is this emergency Board Meeting taking place? Will you be able to attend so you can find out what's going on and answer any accusations?"

"Apparently I'm going to be summoned with *a notice to present myself,* according to Pat. She had a few during her tenure although never for something along this line. She advocates that I don't give an inch."

"Ah, wise woman and I'm sure you'll take her advice."

"Oh I'm ready to do battle. I just wish I knew what it's all about because I hate going in blind."

"You get on with the other Board Members well enough so at least you won't be facing a whole roomful of enemies," Grant reassures her.

"Yes, you're right. A few of them well, we'll never be friends, but I get on okay with all of them. They voted me into the position and they won't want it to seem like they've made a mistake. Now, what were you talking about when I so rudely zoned out?"

Grant gives a little laugh saying: "I was just griping about this new case. We've barely gotten started and we're waiting for confirmation from the Medical Examiner's office as to whether or not it could be murder."

"Oh my! So now it's possibly a murder case? That's a big jump from an accidental overdose, isn't it? How? and why?"

"Happily the *why* isn't a question the police have to answer. Believe me we've got enough work with who and how. The list of suspects is shaping up to be... impressive."

"What, you mean lots of people wanted the victim dead?"

"Yeah, it sounds like she was a menace."

Judith laughs at Grant's use of the word saying it makes her think of the *Dennis the Menace* comics. Glad to enjoy a chuckle Grant clarifies that unfortunately none of Gayle's pranks were innocent, she was a malevolent force.

"You make her sound evil!"

He shrugs saying: "I think she was. Evil exists and it comes in many forms. I know because I've seen it with my own two eyes after so many years in this job."

"Are you getting fed up? With police work, I mean. Thinking of making a change?"

Grant scoots closer to Judith and pulls her in for a one-armed hug. "Nah, I'm just complaining because I've got a sympathetic, albeit distracted, ear to listen to me."

She tilts her face up for a kiss and they both sigh at the pleasure of relaxing into a few sweet moments. When they pull apart Judith nestles against Grant's chest and he inhales the lavender scent of the shampoo in her hair.

"This is nice," he comments. They both sit quietly, enjoying the calm of each other's company.

Judith straightens up saying: "You were young when you joined the police so are you coming up to possible retirement age?"

"Actually anyone with 6 years of pensionable service can retire with some money but I always planned on putting in my twenty-five years. I don't know what I'd do with myself though. I don't have any hobbies and although I do golf and I do ski I'm not an avid sportsman. I'd like to do some travelling but it's kind of a hassle nowadays with all the security checks and getting squashed into small seats on an airplane, plus hotel rooms that never look like what's been advertised, and surcharges added to everything."

"A cruise," says Judith knowingly despite never having left the province. "That way you get to visit several countries but only have one flight."

"Hmm, I always thought an Alaskan cruise sounded interesting–"

Judith interrupts with a decisive *no*. It's obvious she's considered the idea before. "You want to take a Mediterranean cruise, or a Scandinavian one, or any European cruise. All kinds of famous cities so close to each other and all very different. Not like a Caribbean cruise where the places are lovely but all the same.

With a cruise you don't have to worry about train schedules or flights or hotel bookings. No arrangements to fuss over. Back in your own cabin each night, your clothes all hung up in your own closet, all meals provided, plus with all the amenities the cruise ships offer they're a vacation all by themselves."

"I guess I know where we're going for our honeymoon, eh? and what are you going to do with this little monster while we're away?" asks Grant, gently lifting Panda off the couch and onto his lap.

He complains that his clothes are always covered in cat hairs these days yet he's always picking up the little bundle of fur. Judith, always conscious about looking professional, has noticed the same problem and keeps a sticky roller brush at the front door for a quick clean up before heading out. Nevertheless people are always noticing pet hairs and asking *do you have a dog or a cat or both?*

"Don't talk about my Christmas present from you that way," she admonishes, giving the kitten a fond look.

"Will you ask Beth to take care of her?"

"I thought about it but... I think it's too much to ask with a brand-new baby in the house. So I decided to board her and that way we can get her used to going to a kennel whenever we're away."

"Aww, poor little thing stuck in a kennel."

"Actually this place I heard about is no ordinary kennel. It's a home-based business where cats are boarded with the family. I've already spoken to the woman and she explained that for the first few days Panda might be shy and will probably hide from the other cats but by the end of her stay she'll have settled right in.

The only drawback is she has to have a rabies vaccine and I have to produce proof. It's for the protection of the other animals."

"I thought she got all her shots?"

"She did, except rabies. The vet said she didn't need that shot so long as she's always going to be a house-cat and I assured him she will be. I have no interest in taking her out on a leash or anything like that."

"Well, you've got some time before you have to decide. How did you hear about this kennel?"

"From Xiao, you know him, one of the teachers at work. He has two cats, a brother and sister, he inherited when his mother passed away. He's used this service, it's called Kitty's Kozy Kottage and I know it's a silly name but it's certainly easy to remember."

"Don't I remember this Xiao guy being very antagonistic towards you?"

"Oh he sure was!"

"What changed?"

"Marta Smith retiring and moving away. Now that Xiao's gotten out from under her influence he's turned out to be a really great guy. He's funny and fun, gets along with everybody, it's a real change. And it's sure made me realize just how poisonous Marta was with her vindictive nature."

"I'm glad to hear that. But for now... let's forget about other people and just concentrate on you and me for the rest of the evening."

Judith smiles sweetly agreeing that's a wonderful idea.

Rumours

Gayle is on the shoulder of the highway, resigned to having to make her way home on foot. *On these damn high-heeled feet,* she grumbles. Gayle frequently talks to herself, usually out loud. Even though it's her own voice she likes to hear the sound, it gives her company.

Clear nights have become rare in Calgary but it's cold and cloudless now. Gayle tilts her head up looking for the Aurora Borealis. *It's years since I've seen The Northern Lights.* Instead she sees a billion stars and the very vastness of the night sky makes her shiver with a sense of longing, maybe loss.

She's prepared to turn and stick her thumb out if she ever hears a car. Gayle expected to see transport trucks on the highway but there haven't been any vehicles going west at this time on Good Friday night. *Is it still Friday?* she wonders, regretting the fact that she ditched her phone.

After calling in the anonymous tip stating there were drugs in the dressing-room at Heavenly Bodies Gayle panicked about having her call traced. She'd stashed the cocaine in her locker and now she's scared the club's owners will track her down.

Just because that brick is in my locker doesn't prove that I put it there. Any one of those women could have done that. There's no padlock on Gayle's locker. She gave up having one because she could never remember the combination. Anyone who can get in the dressing-room can get in her locker.

Doesn't matter anyhow, she thinks deciding, *I'm not gonna go back there. I can find a better job.*

The dazzling reflection of headlights bouncing from the slight incline in the road catch her attention. Sticking out her arm, thumb cocked in the classic hitchhiking gesture, she turns but has to fling up her other arm to shield her eyes.

The car's lights dim and the vehicle slows, signals, and pulls over a few metres ahead. Gayle hurries up to the car catching hold of the passenger door that the driver has shoved open.

"Hey I'm sorry about the brights!" exclaims a young male voice.

Bending to look inside Gayle sees there's only one person inside. He has the friendly boy-next-door good looks of a young Tom Cruise and Gayle is reassured. Years of dealing with grabby men in a strip club have given her a false confidence that she can take care of herself.

"Thanks for stopping, guy," she says sliding into the seat with a relieved sigh. "My feet are killing me."

"Where are you going to? It's not a good idea to walk along this road late at night, you know."

"Mmm, but I don't have a choice. Somebody stole my purse so I've got no money and no phone." Casting a sidelong look at the driver Gayle sees that he's bought her lie. "I'm going to Edgemont, do you know it? you can drop me at the turn-off, it's just up here a ways."

The boy says he's going to Edgemont himself and he pulls back onto the highway. In a voice filled with indignation and sympathy he asks if she wants to use his phone to call the police.

"Aww you're sweet, but they won't do anything. Especially since I didn't have a lot of money and the phone is old. Besides, all I could tell them is that the person came up behind me on a 10-speed and snatched my bag right off my shoulder. All I saw was a dark hoodie which isn't much of a description. I couldn't even say if it was a man or a woman."

"Well that's really shitty– oh sorry!"

Gayle smiles at him apologizing for such mild swearing and assures him it's quite all right.

"No really, you're older than me so I shouldn't talk disrespectful."

"Just how old do you think I am?" Gayle tilts her head flirtatiously but inside she feels a mix of offended and curious.

With the casual cruelty of youth he guesses: "I dunno about, um... well I think you must be about ten years older than me so twenty-eight?"

"Actually I'm almost thirty," Gayle replies.

The teenager laughs saying: "Oh wow, that's worse, that's even older than I thought!"

Gayle narrows her eyes at the youth thinking: *what a little goof this kid is. These boys... Harry's almost his age and he's another little twerp. Him and his crap car.*

They reach the turn-off for Edgemont and he carefully signals before exiting onto the secondary road. The new shopping centre immediately comes into view and the boy drives to the far end explaining: "I'm picking up my girlfriend from her job at the movie theatre. They have a late show on Friday and Saturday nights."

He's completely unaware that while his cussing meant nothing to Gayle she's insulted by his reaction to her age.

I get hit on by men all the time but here's this punk acting like I'm too old for him? Gayle's temper, inherited from her mother, is always ready to flare from a simmer to a boil but luckily they've arrived in front of the darkened theatre.

The outer door opens and a very young-looking girl hurries out. She reaches for the car-door handle but stops abruptly when she sees Gayle through the window, her eyes and mouth rounded into surprised O shapes.

"You'd better move into the back-seat so Tasha can get in the front," the boy says.

Gayle gets out and steps away calling over her shoulder: "Thanks, I'll walk from here." She blows him a kiss and adds an extra wiggle to her walk when she hears the girl hiss *Who is that?*

Being out in the open again Gayle feels the chill of the night as she walks into the sleeping village of Edgemont. Gayle Boudreau is now less than two hours away from her death.

***

Judith came to work two hours early on Tuesday morning. After a restless night she woke up well before her alarm, anxious to ensure that all trace of the weekend's police presence was removed from the school yard. When she dropped in yesterday afternoon the tape was still up and she'd had to walk right around the school to let herself in the front door.

Now, she's thankful that there's no sign of the police presence or that of the body. Even the cigarette butts have been removed. *Although that might have been Mr. Glover, bless him*, she thinks.

Judith has just sat herself down at her desk to begin the day's work when Samira comes into her office. Judith texted her with a heads-up about the body on Saturday in case Samira heard something and was questioned.

The school secretary has been in the building for more than an hour herself but this is their first meeting today.

"Good Morning, Principal Taylor. I hope you managed to have a good Easter weekend despite everything."

Samira always uses titles. She once explained that the hard work and effort it takes to attain a position should be respected.

"I did, thanks. Lila cooked us an excellent dinner. What about you? I know you don't celebrate Christian religious holidays but there are fun secular things like Easter Egg hunts and a visit from the Easter Bunny."

"To say nothing of the two days off! I'm always willing to celebrate a paid day off," Samira laughs at herself but Judith notices she hasn't said if her children got an Easter basket. "And of course Ramadan starts in a week. Meanwhile, I just had a courier drop off this envelope.

I opened it, it's not marked private or anything, and it's a formal request that you attend a special meeting of the school's Board on Thursday."

She hands the letter to Judith who carefully scans every line.

"This isn't a request, it's a demand. I'm being *commanded to attend* and here they specifically say to answer a serious allegation. It still doesn't spell out what the actual incident of *moral turpitude* is.

Well, well..." she pauses to gather her thoughts. "Do you recall Pat ever getting something like this?"

Samira answers right away that *no, nothing quite like this ever happened with ex-Principal Johnson although she did get several summons from the Board over the years.*

Judith rereads the missive saying: "It's signed by the Board Secretary, but specifically mentions that the complainant is someone called Moira Porter-Wilson. What do we know of her?"

"Just that she's a new Board Member. A vacancy came up when Morag MacKenzie retired and Ms. Porter-Wilson got the appointment."

Speaking her thoughts aloud Judith murmurs "I wish I knew what this is about, I just can't think of anything."

"Principal Taylor... um, I wonder if..." Samira breaks off, hesitant to speak up.

"Please Samira, if you have any inkling please let me know what's on your mind," Judith implores.

"Well it's probably far-fetched but I guess no more then the idea of a *moral turpitude* charge being levelled against anyone here. I just wondered if this new Board Member is talking about Holly Lezinsky's murder? or how the school – not through any fault of ours of course – has been connected to several killings?"

"But we didn't do anything wrong!" exclaims Judith. "However you're right and *mud sticks* as the saying goes. In just over a year, well about sixteen months, we have been involved with the police a lot. Do you think that could be it? It just might be... but why would that warrant an emergency meeting?"

"Oh I don't know if my idea is right, it's just the only possible thing I could think of that a new Board Member might take issue with."

Sitting back in her chair Judith meets Samira's worried gaze and comments: "A *new* Board Member, yes. She might be overly enthusiastic or wanting to make a name for herself. Pat warned me to be firm when dealing with the Board.

Actually your idea would be a great result because I can easily answer that accusation by asking what she thinks we could have - and should have - done differently."

Looking at the summons once again Judith continues: "Let's meet their formality with our own. The Board Secretary is requesting I RSVP so will you please draft a serious-sounding reply of acceptance and send it back in a high priority email?"

"Certainly, Principal Taylor and, if I may, can I suggest I c.c. our lawyer?"

Judith lets out a surprised laugh. "How deviously clever of you, Samira! Yes, by all means do that very thing. The lawyer will charge us something simply for getting an email but it will be worth it if we can rattle the Board's cage a little. That's a wonderful suggestion, thank you!"

Samira nods, accepting the compliment with a slight smile as she leaves to fulfill her task.

**

Reg and Grant are back at the strip club. Like most nighttime entertainment venues it looks somehow wrong in the daylight. The building is non-descript, bland even, without it's colourful neon sign flashing. The big parking-lot is almost deserted and the front doors are propped open. No doubt to air the place out.

It's dim inside with only electric lighting - the windows all painted over in black - and they have to watch their step around the cords of industrial cleaning machines. These are being noisily wielded by a crew of small-stature workers who keep their heads down, but peek up at the detectives and quickly move out of their way.

Grant doesn't know what language they're speaking but it doesn't sound Latino. He figures the crew is probably Eastern European. Not necessarily here illegally but obviously anxious to avoid contact with the police. *Probably because of stories they've heard about interactions with the authorities in their homeland,* he thinks. He has no idea how intimidating he and Reg look standing shoulder-to-shoulder.

The Crown Prosecutor's office came through and the detectives are here to review the surveillance tapes from the inside of Heavenly Bodies on Friday April 2nd from evening until closing.

The agreement says they can only view them here on the premises, no copying, but they can make note of time markers related to incidents. Also the Club can't wipe these tapes and must keep them secure in case they're needed as evidence in court.

The manager, Sol Stein, isn't as affable on this visit and they understand why when he explains there are *a couple of encounters* as he puts it, that need clarification. Neither of the detectives respond as the three of them settle in his office where several big monitors show scenes playing from different angles on each one.

They view the main screen, playing the video at an accelerated pace until Grant signals for Sol to stop the tape, back up, and replay it slowly dryly remarking: "This appears to be one of those conflicts."

The slo-mo frames show Gayle just entering the hallway, a big grin on her face, when suddenly a hand comes into view yanking on her arm. The expression on her face is one of alarm as she's dragged through a doorway and slammed against the wall. It's this office, Sol's office, and it is Sol's hands around Gayle's throat. There's no sound so the police turn to the manager for an explanation.

"Yeah, the way it looks it wasn't really that bad... um, I admit I was angry. I'd just been listening to a load of complaints about how Gayle's been stealing from the other girls, and something about her having sex with one of the bouncers who is already spoken for, and on top of it I'd had to pay for a car to pick her up or she threatened not to show.

So yeah, I was pissed at her and came on pretty strong but I wanted to make sure she knew she was on her last chance with me."

Grant makes a *hmmm* sound and nods for Sol to start up the tape again. They see Sol release Gayle who then hurries down to the dressing-room but there's no camera in there.

They watch how a typical Friday night unfolds inside the strip club. The dancers perform their routines on one screen, the audience are surveilled on another screen, and the hallway leading to the public washrooms, the dressing-room, Sol's office, and a storage area is also shown. They only see dancers enter and leave the dressing-room.

There's an emergency exit sign over a steel door at the end of the corridor but no one comes through it in either direction.

All three men watch Gayle's performance and it's obvious she isn't very acrobatic on the pole or much of a dancer either, but the crowd approves of her sinuous, blatantly sexual movements. She earns plenty of cash and applause.

Once Gayle comes off the stage Sol directs their attention to the video taken of the audience. "There was a bit of a disturbance here..."

Gayle has slipped into a short wrap and now they see her approach a customer who already has a dancer in his lap. Gayle pushes up against him and kisses the bald spot on the top of his head. He tilts his face up to her and their exchange looks flirtatious.

The other dancer leans over the man and roughly shoves Gayle away. She saunters away, hips swaying and laughing, but then a couple of frames later the man jumps from his chair yelling and waving his arms.

Sol pauses the tape and tells them the man is yelling *I've been robbed! My wallet is missing.* Sol starts up the video again and they can see that the girl performing the lap dance isn't wearing enough to hide as much as a business card. Both her and the customer's heads swivel in the direction Gayle went and he points dramatically. Gayle has moved around one of the bouncers who now stands between her and the irate man.

The first girl bends to the ground and they can see her quickly stand triumphantly waving a brown wallet. The customer hurries back and opens it to show it's empty inside.

Again Sol pauses the video and tells the detectives *the dancer confirmed that when the man paid for his lap dance she'd seen several more green $20 bills, and at least one red $50.*

The man isn't young but he looks fit and ready to fight for his missing funds.

Sol explains: "He's a regular customer who drinks plenty and tips well so I gave him one hundred cash and comped his tab for the night as a goodwill gesture.

I didn't want an angry drunk on my hands so I had Jerome put him in a cab. I'm sure we can find out who it was and you can confirm that they took him home. We have a strict policy that those drivers must follow or risk being banned from our business, you see we know what goes on. Most of the drunks will try to get out a block away then walk back for their cars. That's why we insist the cabbies follow our rules.

Anyhow, I can't prove Gayle stole his money but I have no doubt that she did."

"Why didn't you say anything about this before?"

"Randy took the bill I gave him and swore I was his best friend by time we got him out the door. Gayle was still there, she had another set coming up, so there was no more interaction between them. It was all *done and dusted* and I forgot about it."

To say nothing of the fact that the man's a regular who spends freely, thinks Grant.

There aren't any more quarrels that night, just a few men getting their wandering hands smacked by the waitresses, and several by-law infractions for smoking and vaping. To say nothing of the Covid violations.

Sol Stein can be glimpsed on one camera or another all night.

***

Tasha can't concentrate in the classroom. Normally she's an actively engaged student, putting up her hand to ask and to answer questions. Now she's fidgetting, anxiously waiting the ring of the lunch bell. Tasha's desperate to get to her phone so she can text Shane with the news about the body found on the school steps. She only knows what the rumours have said and they're becoming wilder with each retelling.

With only a few minutes to go there's a knock on the door and Principal Taylor enters the room. "I apologize for interrupting your class, Ms. Shapiro," she tells Tanya, "but I want to speak with everyone about the very unfortunate and tragic discovery that was made over the weekend."

The teacher nods and Judith turns to face the girls. She has their eager attention.

"We don't have much in the way of detailed information, but the facts are as follows: the body of an unidentified woman was discovered early on Saturday morning. She was found lying on the back-door steps of the school apparently having died from a drug overdose. The police are investigating the source of the drugs and," she adds dryly, "the victim was found fully clothed."

With a thank you to Tanya Shapiro Judith withdraws, her authority such that no one demands more information or to ask questions. Whispering begins immediately and moments later when the bell rings for the lunchtime break the girls voices rise in excited chatter.

Tasha hurries to her locker to share the news with Shane. He's in his first year at the University and is allowed to carry his phone at all times so he answers her text by calling back right away.

"Yeah we heard about it here. Was she inside the school? is there blood? are the cops there?"

"No, she was found outside, at the back stairs, you know where the parking lot is? And no blood because they said she OD'd."

"Fentanyl?"

"Probably, but nobody knows yet. And there's no police here. That's all Principal T is saying. You know, it's only because on Sunday someone's mother spotted that yellow crime tape they use when she drove home from church that we found out something happened.

That lady called around to other parents and that's how it got out, otherwise nobody would have told us a thing. You know how they like to shelter us."

Shane is disappointed to learn the facts after thinking he was tantalizingly close to a real-life murder. "Drugs? that's so boring,"

"I know, eh?" sticking her head into her locker and pulling the door around herself for privacy Tasha lowers her voice: "But listen Shane, what if the body is that woman hitchhiker you picked up on the highway?"

"Why would it be her?"

"Well, we don't know where she went and you know how she looked, not like someone who lives here, and she was headed in the right direction, like towards the school, when she walked away from us."

Perking up at the idea Shane replies: "Yeah maybe... yeah, it could be her, huh?"

"So I think you should call the cops and tell them about her."

"Oh I don't know if I want to get involved in something–"

"C'mon, you're taking Law so you've got like a responsibility or something don't you?"

"Tash I'm taking Environmental Law not criminal but... maybe I'll mention it in class and see what people think."

Validation from their peers makes perfect sense to Tasha who readily agrees: "Oh yeah, that's a good idea. Let me know, okay?"

"Sure, and you saw her too so if the cops do actually want to talk to me they'll want to talk to you too you know."

"Fine by me," declares Tasha feeling important.

They end their conversation with endearments and a promise on Shane's part to text her once he decides what he's going to do.

The Married Lover

Grant phoned inviting himself to swing by Judith's apartment *for a cup of your wonderful coffee* and now they're sitting at her kitchen table with a plate of cookies to go with their brew.

"How's your case going?"

"I'm frustrated at the time we've lost thinking Gayle Boudreau died from an accidental overdose. It feels like we're playing catch-up and that's no way to run an investigation.

Right now I'm just hanging fire so, since you need a sounding board tell me what's going on with this Board Meeting?"

Grant knows the summons to a critical Board Meeting is preying on Judith's mind and he wants to lend her his moral support. Judith shakes her head and answers: "Nothing," but her teeth are worrying at her bottom lip.

Grant, deciding a diversion is called for, complains: "Babe, my sisters are calling non-stop and driving me up the wall."

At her enquiring look he explains: "They need a date so they can get started on the wedding planning and—"

"Excuse me, but isn't it my wedding?" Judith interrupts indignantly.

"Oh sweetheart," Grant begins with a smile, "No, sorry, but you're marrying into a family of crazy females. No job is too big or too small to escape their attention. They attack every task like they're going for the gold. They will smother you with love and affection so for the sake of your sanity give up and give in."

"Well I don't think I like you acting like it's okay for me to be bossed around–"

Sitting up straight Grant nods stating: "Fair point. Let me know what you've already taken care of and I'll tell them to cross it off their list. Lists, actually."

Being put on the spot flusters Judith as she says: "Well I haven't really..." then seeing his smirk complains: "Oh Grant you know perfectly well I haven't done a darn thing."

Grant thinks her pout is adorable but doesn't dare say so. Trying to keep the laughter out of his voice he continues: "And you don't even know where to begin, right?"

Judith exhales a gusty breath and it carries a burst of anger. "I'm not ready to set a date yet, okay?"

"But... but Judith, why not?" With a panicked look on his face Grant reaches for her hand saying urgently: "You haven't changed your mind about us have you?"

"No! not at all it's just... you'll probably think I'm being silly but I want Lila and Brian to have their day first. See, since they've both been married before and then lost their spouses this time the ceremony will be low-key. I'm afraid our wedding will overshadow their quiet little celebration and I don't want to take anything from them."

"Oh Judith no wonder I fell for you, your kindness just overwhelms me."

"Kindness? No. Empathy, maybe. I'm good at putting myself in someone else's shoes, so to speak."

Relaxing a little Grant leans back in his chair. "So when are they getting married? I can give the sisters a heads-up and that should keep them quiet for a bit." Seeing her face he says: "Uh-oh! what now?"

Judith is back to her nervous habit of chewing on her bottom lip. "Wellll," she draws the word out. "They haven't set a date yet."

"Why not? I thought they were going to get married right away. I know Brian wants to."

"Lila is... I don't know why not! She keeps putting me off when I ask."

"Hon, we can't just keep waiting forever. I want us to be married sooner rather than later. We're ready now." After so many years of being commitment-shy Grant is now eager to start this new chapter in their lives.

"I know, I know." Brightening she adds: "But Lila definitely wants them to be married before the baby comes."

"Okay, when will that be?"

"She's due at the end of July. Lila figures she got pregnant at Hallowe'en."

"Of course she did." Grant's face has taken on a grumpy look. "So, do you think we can safely say they'll marry by the end of May? She won't want to be rolling down the aisle–"

Judith interrupts him with a smack to his arm. "Well, hon if it's going to be a quiet celebration... think about it."

Judith does and when she suddenly bursts out laughing Grant can't help but join her. "The end of July is four months away and my sisters can definitely work with that."

Pulling out his phone he checks the time and says: "I've got to get going. We have an interview this evening at the station."

"Oh, that sounds serious."

"Actually it was her choice to come in. It's a woman who is claiming she has information and is somebody's alibi for Gayle's death."

Standing Grant pulls Judith up from her chair and into his arms. They kiss and when they break apart she gets a saucy look on her face saying: "Well this is the part in mystery books where the detective points out that whoever is giving a suspect an alibi is giving themselves one as well."

"I'll keep that in mind, *Miss Marple*," he laughs.

"Hey! can't you think of somebody younger?"

"Oh sure... *Nancy Drew*."

"Ha! Now you're showing your age. I was thinking *Rebekah, Girl Detective*."

***

Grant and Reg are seated in the same interview room they used yesterday. As Reg sets up the recording equipment he murmurs *déja vu?* and Grant nods in agreement. This time Reg is going to start the interrogation.

They are here again because a woman called Cindy Grubowski phoned for an appointment saying she wanted to make a statement. Her name hasn't show up in relation to Gayle Boudreau in any way they know of, so they're intrigued to hear what she has to say. If she was a time-wasting *crime groupie* she would have just shown up at the front desk unannounced.

The door is ajar and knocking lightly a patrolman pushes it open, ushering their visitor inside. Both Grant and Reg stand as a professionally courteous gesture, but this woman would bring any man to his feet.

Cindy Grubowski is a tall redhead whose long hair cascades in waves over a voluptuous figure. Her gorgeous face is made-up discreetly, and her dress is modest, but nothing can dim her feminine beauty.

Grant pulls out a chair for her while Reg simply stares and the patrolman hovers in the doorway.

"And this is Mr. Grubowski," the young policeman says, drawing a man forward. Both detectives are disappointed to realize he's way too young to be Cindy Grubowski's father.

She pushes the next chair out from the table and he sits beside her. He wears the bad boy look like a costume. Leather jacket, scruff darkening his jaw, and a sulky expression on his face. None of the men in the room thinks he deserves to have snagged this breathtaking woman.

Grant takes the sign-in sheet and thanking the officer closes the door. Glancing at the information neatly printed he introduces himself to Cindy and Clay Grubowski, confirms their address, and passes the sheet with contact numbers over to Reg.

The vision sits up straight and all three men lean in to hear what she has to say. "I'll start first and then my husband can give you his story.

First off, you should know that I met Gayle Boudreau when I worked as an exotic dancer at Heavenly Bodies. That's how I met Clay, too. Well, I actually met him when I rented a carpet cleaner from his store but it wasn't until he came to visit me at work that we really got to know each another."

Grant figures Cindy Grubowski probably never needed to actually dance or perform any kind of routine. She could simply have walked on stage, taken off her clothes, and raked in the money. From the half-smile on Reg's face it looks like his partner is imagining the very same thing.

"Anyways, Gayle Boudreau or *Lady L'Amour* as she liked to be called, was nothing but trouble. She stole! none of us had much, but if I bought a new nail polish? Gone! if Gayle was anywhere in the vicinity. Just little things like that, but it was annoying and a lousy thing to do, too.

The worse thing was how she couldn't keep her hands off other people's boyfriends. The poor men couldn't help themselves. I mean, she was pretty and she was lively but most of all she sure was sexy."

Grant feels his eyes widen in surprise at this comment from a woman who embodies sex appeal.

"When I found out she'd gotten her hooks into Clay I was mad and I was hurt. He begged me to forgive him and eventually I agreed but only if there was no more messing around. Because I knew that's all it was with Gayle.

See I knew she didn't want Clay, not on a permanent basis, but she did want to take him away from me. If I'd kicked him out she'd have lost interest. That's just the way she was. It was weird.

I thought things were over between them but turns out..." here she turns to face her husband and with narrowed eyes and a curled lip she continues: "I was wrong. He says it was just one more time but I'm not sure I believe that—"

Clay Grubowski finally comes to life as he grabs his wife's hands to rub his thumbs over them, as if this massage will make his earnest plea more believable.

"Cindy sweetheart, I swear. I didn't even realize what was happening until we were doing it. I know, I know that sounds crazy-stupid but it was all so fast and once I realized I pushed her away but by then, apparently, the damage was done."

The skeptical look on Reg's face mirrors Grant's expression. The older man asks: "Were you involved with Ms. Boudreau at the time of her death?"

"No! No, not at all. We were finished, I broke it off just like I told Cindy I would, but yeah, there was just that one other time..." he's reluctant to go on but his wife prompts him.

"Tell them about how you saw her on that Friday, the Friday she died."

"Friday April 2nd? Good Friday?"

"Yeah, the store was open because we're always busy when people have a day off so I was working and Gayle came by."

After a half-minute of silence Grant loses his patience. "I don't like having to pull this story out of you word-by-word, Mr. Grubowski. Please just make your statement and we'll stop you when we have questions."

"C'mon, Clay. The only thing you were worried about was me finding out and I found out anyhow so just go ahead and explain it all."

Exhaling loudly the man rubs his hand over his mouth and then tells his story.

"Gayle came into the shop as happy as if she'd just won the lottery. Her eyes were shiny and her hair bounced because she was kinda skipping instead of walking. She was in a great mood because she enjoyed ruining other people lives. She was loud and sassy, all hyped-up, making wild claims, making demands, and I wanted to shut her up and I, well, I um... slapped her."

A look of shame settles on the man's face. Reg and Grant exchange a glance, both wondering if the man is this embarrassed by the fact he struck a woman how likely is it that he actually killed her?

"You and your wife have voluntarily come in together today, which we appreciate, but frankly the state of your marriage is not our business. You need to spell out exactly what these demands entailed and then convince us you didn't kill the woman–"

"Kill? The news said Gayle died of a drug overdose!" Cindy interjects, obviously shocked.

"The Medical Examiner hasn't yet given us a definitive cause of death but there are some suspicious elements – questions we need to answer. Getting back to you Clay, was Gayle Boudreau blackmailing you over your affair?"

"Affair? No, we were over, no chance of me getting with her again," the man's mouth twists in a sneer. "No, all Gayle wanted was some money. She volunteered to have an abortion if I would pay–"

"Wait, what? Gayle was pregnant?"

"You guys didn't know?"

"We don't have the autopsy report back yet. Again, we're waiting on the Medical Examiner. The office is short-staffed because of the Easter long weekend." Reg is discomfited by the news. Not knowing about the pregnancy has put them at a disadvantage.

Clay is unaware of dropping a bomb and goes on to explain: "I had no reason to kill her because all Gayle wanted was money and I agreed to pay her."

"Are you sure she was pregnant?"

"She showed me a test result, she knew I wouldn't pay up without proof. I mean, the test only proved she was pregnant, not that it was mine necessarily. But she knew I wouldn't want Cindy, my wife, to hear about it which meant I wouldn't drag things out by fighting her over it."

"Abortions are free under Alberta Healthcare."

"Yeah, I know, but Gayle said she'd be off work for awhile afterwards. So after a bit of back and forth we agreed on an amount. I have the money, that wasn't a problem, she knew I was good for it."

Reg gives him a skeptical look. "And what about when she came back for more?"

"Well... what could she do then? She wouldn't be pregnant no more, she'd have nothing to threaten me with, and... I might have scared her off coming around again..." he trails off miserably at the implication of what he's saying.

Leaning forward Reg states: "Yet it seems you did come clean with your wife after all?"

"Oh no, Detective. Clay thought he'd gotten away with it. It was one of the employees at the shop who phoned me right away and gave me the whole story. He said he was *telling me as a friend*,"

Clay snorts and she pauses to incinerate him with her glare. "He said he thought *I should know what was going on behind my back*. I'll be honest with you, I was hurt, sure, but really angry too. Angry at Clay."

"Not Gayle?"

"Gayle was just being Gayle. I mean yeah, I thought she was trash, but she's not the one who broke a vow to be faithful to me. That was all Clay."

No one speaks while they consider Cindy's words. Finally Reg says: "You told us you and Gayle had reached a financial agreement so she left and then what? Take us through the rest of your day."

"Well by then it was just past quitting time. We close at 6:00 on holidays and weekends so it would have been fifteen to twenty minutes after that by time I locked up and left."

"Clay always texts when he's on his way. He didn't have time to make a detour, believe me I was watching the clock ready to lay into him. He came straight home."

Cindy produces her phone and scrolling back to the day in question shows the men a 6:16 message from a contact called *Hubby*.

"You got home and... fireworks?" asks Grant.

Clay winces and nods. As the two detectives give the recorder a pointed look he hastens to say *yes*.

With a desperate look on his face he says: "You gotta believe me! I had no reason to kill Gayle, I wouldn't anyhow. I'm not a killer and Gayle well, Gayle wasn't worth the risk. I had enough of a scare thinking I'd lost my wife because of her."

"Clay! we talked about this!" Cindy interjects.

"Sorry! I should have said because of me. It was my fault, not Gayle's. But I fixed it. I fixed it with money, not killing.

I got home, Cindy ripped me a new one, I grovelled and, thank God, she forgave me. I didn't leave the house again until I went into work Saturday morning."

"Hmm. The only corroboration to this comes from your wife."

"But Cindy, I'm inclined to believe that you're telling the truth," adds Grant and Reg nods his agreement.

"Okay Clay. Just sit tight until we get this statement written up for you to sign. Do either of you want a coffee or anything?"

"No, nothing. Thanks."

The room seems strangely empty when the two big cops leave. Clay leans his elbows on the table and rests his face in the palms of his hands, eyes closed.

The strain from this conversation shows on Cindy's face, and she subconsciously shifts in her seat until she's slightly turned away from her husband.

Observing them through the one-way glass Reg asks Grant what he thinks.

"This news of Gayle's pregnancy adds a whole new layer of complication to the case, doesn't it? We need to find out who, if anyone, knew about it, and did she try to extort money from anyone else?

It means our suspect list has just grown. There's this married boyfriend and his wife who also knew the victim and disliked her. Maybe Cindy did blame Gayle and hated her for trying to break up their marriage?

Plus, there's Eric Littner. Gayle was actually living with him while running around with Clay Grubowski, but did he know that? Littner's statement puts him in the clear however now that we're considering homicide we'll have to carefully check up on his alibi.

As for Clay here, I don't *think* he killed her, but I'm not ready to cross him off the suspect list yet." Grant stays watching the couple while Reg takes the tape away for transcription.

The appeal on the nightly news for anyone with information to come forward has certainly paid off. Of course once word gets out that it's now a suspicious death people will be less likely to voluntarily get involved.

Young Witnesses

A day-and-a-half's worth of texts discussing, phone calls arguing, and in-person crying then reconciling, result in Tasha and Shane showing up at the Police Station.

Munez is back on duty and he listens carefully while studying the teenagers. The two aren't telling their story well, they keep interjecting and interrupting each other, but the Desk Sergeant just nods while they ramble.

In his mind he thinks *badly dressed, but in expensive clothes. They're obviously rich Edgemont kids.* Having come to this conclusion he doesn't fob them off requesting they submit a written report but instead rings through to the Detectives' Room.

When Reg answers Munez explains that a couple of potential witnesses regarding the Boudreau case have come in to make a statement... possibly.

"Well, well you must have been a good boy in another life Grant, because we've got another walk-in witness. Two of them, actually and they sound interesting. I'll go fetch them and meet you in the interview room."

"Nice to be popular," smiles Grant as he follows Reg out.

Grant has just finished setting up the recording device when Reg comes in with a big grin on his face. His good humour is explained when he shepherds in two kids and sees Grant's unguarded expression. Both detectives school their faces into polite masks as they ask if the couple would like coffee or water before they begin.

The youth shakes his head *no* but the girl asks: "What kind of sparkling water do you have?"

And when Grant deadpans: "Tap." She wrinkles her nose saying she's changed her mind.

Reg briskly gets the proceedings underway. The boy is called Shane Piett and the girl is Natasha *(eww, call me Tasha)* DeMong. He's eighteen years old and she's seventeen, both are residents of Edgemont. He's studying at the University of Calgary and she attends Edgemont School for Girls.

Reg has done his best to extract this information with a minimum of off-topic chat. He can see Grant looking slightly shell-shocked at the barrage of inane commentary. Plus Grant is distracted by their touchy-feely behaviour.

The couple appear incapable of keeping their hands off each other. Constantly leaning in to touch arms, bumping shoulders, his knee rubbing against her leg, her foot tapping on his. Reg, having raised a family, is used to this behaviour from teens.

They explain they've come to the Police Station because *we think Shane picked up the drug overdose woman hitchhiking late on Friday night.*

"So can you describe this woman and where you picked up? how was she dressed and–"

"Picking up hitchhikers is never a good idea," puts in Grant, not sure why he's feeling censorious.

Reg smoothly brings the conversation back adding: "While that's true I can understand your concern seeing a lone woman walking late at night, son."

Shane straightens up in his chair and shifting his body closer to Tasha turns all his attention to Reg. "I just thought *what if it was Tasha who was stranded?* and knew I had to help her."

"You'd never leave me to walk by myself," declares Tasha with a shove.

"But what if I was late coming to get you and you gave up waiting and started walking?"

"Well I'm not stupid, I wouldn't walk alone at night, I'd call Daddy to come and get me. Besides you're never late picking me up—"

"I could be in a car accident."

"Shane! Don't say stuff like that, it's bad luck!"

Interrupting the boy's move to comfort her with yet another cuddle Reg regains their attention, reminding them he needs a description and a location.

Leaning forward Tasha delivers a scathing report. "She looked really trashy, you know hair really dry from overbleaching, really obvious fake eyelashes, a really low-cut short dress, tight, and just a little jean jacket."

A really little jean jacket? thinks Grant sarcastically.

Shane enthusiastically agrees adding: "And boots so high—"

"He means heels so high, on her boots," interjects Tasha.

"Yeah, that. I don't know how she walked in them. I found her just before the first exit into Edgemont."

"But omigod, those boots, bleech! Bright red, really flashy, they sure looked like stripper boots," she confirms.

Grant considers the puritanical judgement of youth while he and Reg wordlessly communicate their thought that these two definitely did meet up with Gayle Boudreau the night she died. Time to get serious.

Reg pulls out his notebook and does his best to pinpoint the time Shane picked the woman up until she left his car. Tasha adds such details as *her perfume was so strong and stinky, like musky or maybe that was because of how it mixed with her sweat.*

"If we show you some photos of clothing do you think you could identify–"

"We can look at the body if you want, right Shane?"

"Oh! well, Shane could because he's an adult but you can't Natasha, I mean Tasha, you're too young."

"Well that sucks. I'm really way more observant than he is."

"Nevertheless... perhaps we could start with photos." Opening a file folder Grant carefully turned photos of the deceased upside down before selecting a couple that show Gayle's clothing laid out on a table in the lab.

Turning them around for the young people to see Tasha is definite, and Shane is *pretty sure about the dress because it's the right colour.* There is no hesitation when they look at the picture of vinyl over-the-knee boots with a thick sole and high heel.

"Oh yeah, those are hers for sure."

"Yup, 100 percent."

"So... we did pick up the dead woman, right? Was she a junkie? She wasn't really skinny."

"Um, there's no evidence of that. Now you've stated she left you no more than ten minutes after midnight. How can you be so sure of the time?"

Tasha is surprisingly clear and precise as she explains the timing of the late show: "Friday night's movie had a runtime of one hour and forty-two minutes. It started at 10:00 and had the usual six minutes of ads and coming attractions so that meant it ended at 11:48.

Now, when the last show starts we wait for thirty minutes and then begin cleaning up the refreshments area. That means emptying out the popcorn machines, pulling up covers over the candy section, wiping down the counters, you know, stuff like that. Almost nobody ever comes out to buy more food that far into the show and if they do, well... we're closed.

Once the movie ends we turn up the lights and hustle people out so we can go along the aisles to clean up the mess of food boxes and drink cups. Sometimes other nasty stuff, too," she adds with a knowing look. Grant doesn't dare meet Reg's eye or he'll burst out laughing.

See we really want to get it all done so when the show ends we can get out quick since they'll only pay us until twelve. We still have clock out though. It's a fingerprint scanner in the Employee Lounge. That's where we put our personal stuff like, you know, coats and things.

So I went and got my jacket and signed out and it was 12:04 and I remember thinking *we got done in less than five minutes*. I'd just got as far as the front door when Shane pulled up so I came straight out to the car. Maybe a minute later."

"Yeah and I told the woman she'd have to move to the backseat so Tasha could sit up front with me but when she got out of the car she just left–"

"Wait, she left you at the theatre?"

"Yeah, she got out and said *thanks* and walked away."

"She had this really fake walk, too," adds Tasha critically.

Both of the men are surprised and dismayed to hear this. They'd assumed Shane would be able to tell them where he dropped Gayle off, not that she walked somewhere in the village.

"What direction did she go? Did you drive by her on the way to Tasha's house?"

"No. I went back to the highway to take the second exit for Edgemont because it saves a lot of time instead of all the stop signs and speed bumps and the slow speed limit between the mall and the Estates."

The Edgemont Executive Estates was an exclusive and expensive subdivision in a village already full of the well-to-do. The second exit was built for the convenience of the Estates inhabitants.

"The theatre is the last building so when she walked down the side she was going straight onto the sidewalk."

"There are some low-rise apartments there, a seniors' residence I think," put in Reg.

"Yeah and on the other side of the road there's the woods."

The four of them spend a moment imagining Gayle click-clacking in her high-heeled boots along the dark, deserted street.

The detectives thank the young couple for coming forward and helping their investigation. Reg offers to drive them home but Shane's parents gifted him a car when he graduated high-school so *I have my own wheels but thanks anyhow,* the teen politely says.

The two detectives return to their office. Grant assumes his usual thinking position of leaning back in his chair while Reg drums his fingers on top of the file folder.

"They could be lying about Gayle walking away from them."

"And teenagers would be more likely to use the school as a venue to get high."

"True that," replies Reg before grinning and adding: "But I really, really, really don't think so, you know?"

***

When the Board of the Edgemont School for Girls meets they always choose a restaurant as their venue. That way they can enjoy a good meal while first discussing, and then voting on, the items in the agenda. Since the school is private and the board members are volunteers no one can tell them how – or where – to conduct their business.

For this meeting they expect a full turn-out and have hired a conference room at The Centre. Lila's involvement with The Edgemont Activity Centre enabled her to get detailed information about the booking.

She walks down the hall from her office to Judith's to pass on what she's heard. Lila knows her friend is deeply concerned about this emergency meeting although Judith tries to play it down. Lila wishes she could attend to stand up beside her.

Lila greets the School Secretary, Samira Kanji, saying: "Hi Samira, how are you?"

"I'm good, Nurse Morelli, and you are looking very well yourself." Samira always addresses the staff formally, same as she does with the Principal. Her explanation to Judith *that titles are earned and deserve respect* applies to everyone with a professional designation. The rest get a courteous Mister, Missus, or Miz.

"I've been good, no morning sickness at all," she raps on the secretary's desk saying *touch wood* then adds: "So far the only drawback is this constant urge to pee. All. The. Time."

Samira chuckles, remembering her own pregnancies. "Principal Taylor is free now if you wanted a word."

"Come on in, Lila," calls Judith from the inner office. "What's up?"

"Nothing urgent, I just heard some news about the Board Meeting from my friend at The Centre and wanted to pass it on. They've requested seating and refreshments of coffee, tea, and water, for sixteen to eighteen attendees, and booked the room for two hours."

"Eighteen? But there are only ten board members and one is on a year-long sabbatical so that's double the actual number. Who else could be coming?"

"I have no idea, but why don't you ask Pat? Maybe she's been invited?" suggests Lila.

Judith agrees saying she'll call Pat tonight and let Lila know what she says. Then she changes her mind, realizing she can't bear to wait several hours, and there's no point trying to hide her anxiety from her friend.

"No, I'm going to phone her right away. Stay and listen, if you like," she says while clicking on Pat's name in her phone contacts.

"Judith!" the woman answers in her usual booming voice. "Your ears must be burning because I was just talking to Mark about you and this darned Board Meeting that's coming up. Remember? I called you on Good Friday after I heard about it from Jane? My friend Jane Branston?

Anyhow, I just found an email sitting in my Junk folder – been there for days – and it's an invitation for me to attend as *an observer* – that bit's underlined – which I guess means I don't get a vote."

"Pat, Lila tells me they're planning on having up to eighteen in attendance. Any idea who all is coming?"

"I can't say for sure who's coming, but I do know who's been invited. The idiot woman didn't *blind cc* her group email so each of the recipients got everyone's name and address. Which is probably a violation of our stupid Privacy Law. If this Moira person ticks me off I'll just mention that.

Anyhow, I was just telling Mark they've even invited all the inactive members, too! See, the members don't really retire and can always be called on, but they're under no obligation to show up of course. However that phrase, *moral turpitude*, just smacks of something salacious and that's always a draw. But I'll bet they all show up because they'll figure a battle is brewing and everyone enjoys a good cat-fight."

"If you're trying to scare me it isn't working, in fact the opposite is true."

"Good! I'll definitely be there to back you. I might not have a vote but I've got snorting loudly in contempt down to an art form." Pat's deep laugh makes Judith smile too.

Turning serious she continues: "Although I just discovered the email, stupid system sorting my messages for me," she mutters as an aside. "They actually gave everyone plenty of notice so this isn't some knee-jerk reaction... I just wish we knew what it's all about."

"Me too," Judith fervently replies.

She wishes she could discuss her concerns with Grant but he's gone back to that strip club in the city to interview the dancers and bouncers.

Once again Judith finds herself feeling sorry that a young woman has died, but... she selfishly resents how that death involves her school.

Judith wholeheartedly wishes Gayle Boudreau hadn't moved back to Edgemont. Then, the case would have stayed in Calgary where it belongs.

***

Reg's eyes are bright with merriment and his lips quirk up into a smile watching Grant struggle with the dancers. The handsome detective unsuccessfully tries to fend off their advances. The girls aren't *backward about coming forward,* as the saying goes, and he's got his hands full – literally – when they crowd him.

He keeps inching back, away from the aggressive women, until he moves slightly behind Reg's shoulder. With a laugh the older man tells the girls *back off, he just got engaged.* But they're enjoying the game now and when one exclaims: "We'll throw him a bachelor party!" another quickly adds: "Here in the dressing-room, right now!"

"C'mon, ladies. Time to get serious. We've got evidence indicating Gayle Boudreau's fatal dose might have been deliberately administered–" a few gasps greet this news with one woman stating: "We were told it was an accidental overdose."

"It looked that way, possibly by design, which is why we've got questions," Grant adds. He's relieved that the dancers have settled into their chairs and stopped their teasing. His good looks are rarely a drawback but these women, in this environment, make him uncomfortable.

Glancing down at the print-out of stage names that Sol gave them he rolls his eyes but doesn't dare risk a joke. *"Café Noir, Dani Delite, Jordan Juggs, Juicy Lucy, Kitty Kat, Lady L'Amour,* and *Sweet Marie.* I know Gayle was *Lady L'Amour* but that's it. There are five of you here so someone's missing. Can you please identify who's who and give us your real names?"

"Café Noir quit like five-six months ago, and I never knew her name."

"Joanne, but that's all I know. Solly can tell you the rest. I'm *Kitty Kat* and my real name is Stella Leung," says the platinum-haired Asian.

Sitting next to her is *Dani Delite,* neé Carrie McCormick, and the next girl is unmistakably *Jordan Juggs,* aka Alison Boccia. On the other side of the dressing-room are two empty chairs beside a redhead who gives them a finger wave saying: "I'm *Juicy Lucy* and my real name is Lucy Lincoln."

The last spot belongs to an Indigenous woman with pink-streaked hair past her hips. "I'm Donna Starblanket and I go by *Sweet Marie."*

Reg has taken down all the names in his notebook but it's Grant Alison addresses when she asks: "You should probably take down my phone number, too. You can call me anytime."

Her smile is met with a serious look. She gives an exaggerated sigh that thrusts her chest out further saying: "You can't blame a girl for trying."

Pressing his lips tightly together to hide his smirk Reg has to look away. He feels Grant's suspicious gaze on him but he keeps his eyes glued to his notes.

"Right, well. At this stage of our investigation we're gathering information. For example, was Gayle a known drug user? Was she especially friendly with any customers who were dealing? Who are the dealers here?"

When his questions are met with blank stares he continues: "Listen, we aren't with the Drugs Squad but somehow Gayle got hold of tainted product so please, tell us what you know."

The women all murmur that they don't know anything without even exchanging a glance at each other. Grant and Reg had discussed what questions they'd ask on the drive over to the club and both figured any drugs on the premise would be distributed by the motorcycle gang. Neither of them are surprised when none of the dancers are willing to point the finger.

In the lengthy silence that follows Lucy Lincoln speaks up saying: "Look Detectives, you might as well know the truth and that is that Gayle didn't have any friends here. She didn't want to be friends, not with us and not with the customers. She worked here for a long time and it was just a job to her."

Another girl chimes in saying: "Yeah, she never bothered learning new routines, her costumes were uninspired, and she rushed through her lap dances–"

"She chewed gum when she was on stage!" cries Carrie and the others share her indignation.

"Was she dating anybody that you know of?"

"Dating? yeah no, that's not what Gayle did. She only showed interest in a guy if he was involved with someone else. She was always making a play for our boyfriends and husbands, even customers. If any of them showed a preference for a certain dancer she'd try to muscle in on it. Otherwise she wouldn't give the men the time of day."

"Uh-huh, she was weird like that."

"No, what's weird is how she got herself pregnant. She must have–" but Donna is interrupted by shouts and squeals ranging from of *no way!* and *was she really?* to *whose was it?* and *how do you know?* from the other women.

Looking at the policemen Donna asks: "Uh-oh... did you know?"

"We were told she was, but it's yet to be confirmed by the Medical Examiner."

"Well I caught her coming out of the bathroom with the strip in her hand and she told me. Her face was dead white with shock so she didn't get pregnant on purpose."

"What do you mean a strip? I thought you had to pee on a stick to get results?" asks Stella.

"Stick or strip, either works, but the strips are cheaper so it makes sense Gayle would buy one of those tests. Oh what am I saying? she would have shoplifted it so the strip packet must have been the smallest and easiest to get ahold of."

"Did Gayle say anything when you saw her? Did she identify the father? or mention what she planned to do?"

"No, not to me. We weren't friendly with each other. I know she had two boyfriends at the time and one was married. If he was the one who knocked her up she'd probably pretend it was the single guy - if she wanted to get married, that is. Or maybe she'd try to break up the other guy's marriage? Anything's possible where Gayle's concerned but *follow the money* is generally a safe bet when it comes to her."

Both Grant and Reg are thinking about Eric Littner's very expensive car, his nice apartment, and his lucrative career.

"If she was going to keep the baby what would happen with her job here?"

"Oh she'd rake in the money! Believe it or not guys love seeing pregnant strippers. A big belly and swollen boobs? oh yeah, she'd make good money but afterwards her body wouldn't be much good for stripping any more.

I mean some women can do it, Alison and Lucy you both have kids, don't you? but you guys worked hard to lose the baby fat and take care of the marks. I can't see Gayle putting in that kind of effort."

Grant looks at Reg who puts his notebook away with a shrug. Grant nods, acknowledging that they aren't going to learn anything more. Thanking the women the two men leave with whistles, cat-calls, and a suggestion that Grant *walk slowly* following them out the door. The hallway echos with girlish giggles.

"Soooo," says Reg with a grin, "What are you going to tell Judith?"

"There's nothing to tell," snaps Grant with a stern look at his partner. Unabashed Reg laughs outright and continues chuckling all the way to the car.

An Urgent Meeting

Every day this week Harry has met up with Beth at her school or on the walk she takes home. Didi joined them the first day but preferred her clutch of giggling girlfriends. Harry started holding hands with Beth after that.

He sees her to her door but doesn't come in. He has to leave to put in a couple of hours at his part-time job at the car wash. Harry is working to build up a savings account.

He's never travelled beyond Calgary in one direction and Banff in the other and he wants to explore his options beyond the confines of the Edgemont Trailer Park. Ideally, he's hoping to travel from one end of Canada to the other. Working his way east to the Atlantic ocean then coming back west till he reaches the Pacific. He wants to travel with an open mind, looking for a place to call home, though he suspects he'll end up right back here in Alberta.

He's shared his dream with Beth who tells him she plans to go to University right after high-school. "I want to be finished with school, I don't want to take a gap year and drag it out. I want to get my degree, get a job, and then I want to travel."

"You've got goals, eh? That's a good thing. So, what are you planning to study, what type of work do you want to do, and where do you want to travel to?"

Laughing Beth replies: "You probably think you've stumped me but nope, I've got answers to all those questions. I want to qualify as a Pediatric Social Worker, I want to get a job at Sick Kid's Hospital, and I want to travel extensively through Great Britain.

I want to kiss the Blarney Stone in Ireland, and catch a sunrise at Stonehenge in England. I want to walk the Marine Drive Toll Road at Great Orme in Wales, and I want to visit Rosslyn Chapel you know, from the Da Vinci Code? it's in Scotland. Plus all the castles and cathedrals and museums from one end of the British Isles to the other."

"Wow, I'm impressed by every single thing you just said! First off, what kind of a job would you be doing?"

"Oh, lots of different things: patient advocacy, being a liaison with the medical experts, helping families apply for programmes and funding, and counselling.

I'd like to specialize on the children's oncology ward but I found out that I'll have to be accepted for a summer placement first, to make sure I'm a good fit and can handle it, because there will be stressful situations."

"I guess... I can't imagine doing something like that. It'll be really hard won't it?"

"Harder for the kids who are living it. If I can make things easier for them well, I have to try."

"You're a strong girl, Beth Penner."

As they walk along Harry thanks her for cheering him up. "I was feeling kinda down today because I've been worried. It's been a few days since my family learned about Gayle being murdered and things aren't good at home. My mother is constantly fighting with Norm, even though no one believes for one minute that he had anything to do with Gayle's death. It just seems like Mom wants to have arguments."

"Do you think maybe she's feeling... I don't know, guilty or something? because her daughter has died? and maybe she's having a weird reaction or something?"

"Maybe... but Gayle was all grown up. She always did her own thing. Besides, Mom's started picking on me and Didi too, now."

"That's hard on you," Beth sympathizes.

"Aw, I can take it but Didi well... I worry about her. She's sad, and... you know, grieving. Even though Gayle wasn't very nice to her, but she's young and so trusting. Too trusting for someone so pretty and it makes her um.. what's the word?"

"Gullible? Vulnerable?"

"Yeah, both! And that's what she is."

Beth sees that Harry really is concerned and tries to reassure him promising: "You know she's perfectly safe while she's at our school. And when we go to other schools for track meets that aren't girls-only, well none of them are actually, I'll keep an eye out for her."

He nudges her with his shoulder saying: "You're really nice, Beth. You're kind and smart and confident... and beautiful. If you wanna, maybe we could go to a movie some time?"

Beth blushes prettily when she answers: "I'd like that. I like you, Harry."

He grins back but then his expression becomes sombre when he explains: "We'll have to wait a bit 'cause we don't know what's happening with Gayle and, well a funeral and stuff."

Beth doesn't say anything, she just gives his hand a squeeze and instead of breaking apart a block from her home this time he hangs on the rest of the way.

***

Thursday rolls around and Judith is anxious to get to the meeting and find out what's going on. She's been unable to put it out of her mind so a week's worth of wondering has made her edgy and tense. She's finally going to learn what this *moral turpitude* accusation is all about and despite going in blind she's ready to fight.

Judith studies her reflection critically. Most of these women – there are no men on the Board – are wealthy and she can't use her clothing to compete so has opted for an understated, professional look.

Her light gray suit and pale pink blouse are a muted version of the school's uniform. All of the jewellery she's wearing are gifts from Grant: emerald and diamond stud earrings and her engagement ring. Wearing basic make-up, and with her hair simply curled up at the ends, Judith is satisfied with her appearance.

She's never been one for artifice or pretense and secretly has always wondered how on earth she caught the eye of such a handsome man as George Grant. Judith knows other women think the same from the sidelong looks she gets when the two of them are out together.

"Wish me luck Peachy-Pandakins," she tells the cat who pretends she can't hear, her pride refusing to acknowledge this ridiculous new nickname.

Judith believes that being on time means you're late so she arrives at The Centre early enough to park, find the proper room, and be there seven minutes in advance of the appointed hour.

The door is open and the sound of women's voices echoes down the hall, drowning out the click of Judith's heels. Standing in the entrance she pauses for a moment to assess the room. While some of the women are her age the majority, by far, are older ladies.

Eleanor Frampton is present and seeing her gives Judith confidence. She has a lot of respect for the elderly woman who steps forward with her hand outstretched firmly stating: "Judith! I'm delighted to see you again."

People take notice of this encounter and when Pat Johnson greets her *protégée* it's with a grin and a decisive nod. Before anyone else can say anything a tall blonde commands attention with a call for everyone to be seated.

Judith studies her thinking to herself, *This must be Moira Porter-Wilson. Hmm, she's older than me and every inch a proper lady. She looks like she's come straight here from a day's pampering at an exclusive health spa. Every hair in place, make-up perfect, outfit expensive, and ooh I love those shoes! I hate her already.*

Ignoring the order Pat Johnson pulls forward a comfortable-looking woman who she introduces to Judith as *my very good friend Jane Branston*. A pair of intelligent blue eyes twinkle at Judith. She's relieved to discover there are a few allies – or at last open-minded members – in attendance.

Judith is careful to school her face into an expression of listening calm. In order to look interested, but not particularly engaged, she has to hide the thoughts active in her mind and the emotion stirring her blood. She does an excellent job of concealing her impatience while the Board Secretary reads through the last meeting minutes.

Fortunately all the Board's usual protocols are waived in honour of this special urgent meeting. It isn't necessary to stand while speaking but Ms. Porter-Wilson rises to her feet, garnering attention and making sure to draw all eyes to herself.

After introducing herself to the gathering she thanks everyone for attending then jumps right into it. "I realize I'm very new to this Board but we've all heard the adage *a new broom sweeps clean* and, as a newcomer to this vitally important position, I do, I hope, bring a fresh, unbiased perspective." An elderly voice asks *why is she talking about brooms?* but is quickly shushed by her seat-mates.

Ms. Porter-Wilson frowns at the interruption then dives straight into her attack. "It has come to my attention that Lila Morelli, the School Nurse, is expecting a baby and she isn't married," the last phrase is uttered in a voice of harsh contempt. "What kind of an example does that set for impressionable and innocent young girls?"

Judith thinks *that's what this is all about?* and her shoulders slump with relief. A loud snort that she credits to Pat Johnson elicits a wave of giggles until Ms. Porter-Wilson sharply insists this isn't a laughing matter.

Before Judith can reply Jane Branston speaks up saying: "Moira dear, if you believe our girls to be impressionable I simply have to ask: have you met any of them?"

One woman laughs out loud while another claims to know Lila Morelli from her volunteer work and understands that the wedding is happening very soon.

Eleanor asks Judith if that's true and she replies: "Yes, that's correct although I don't see how it's any of the Board's business." She has to raise her voice to speak over Ms. Porter-Wilson's objections.

"Lila Morelli was hired as the School Nurse and she does that job very well. That's all that should matter here."

"Her competence isn't the issue–" begins Ms. Porter-Wilson but Judith cuts her off insisting: "It's the only issue the Board can judge her on. She's not the school's Spiritual Advisor and neither are you, no offence but none of you are."

In an annoying tone of condescension Ms. Porter-Wilson gives Judith a half-smile saying: "I've been told you're very new to the position of Principal, only recently appointed I believe?"

"That's true, and? What point are you trying to make?"

"Well, just that I would expect someone as inexperienced as yourself would be grateful and appreciate the advice from your Board. We really can't have unwed mothers in positions of authority at the school so Miss Morelli should be put on immediate leave."

Now Judith stands so she can look Ms. Porter-Wilson in the eye: "No! Nurse Morelli only has a limited amount of maternity leave and she's hoping to work as long as possible before starting it."

"I'm sorry to hear you say that," the woman answers slowly shaking her head. "It's perfectly clear to me that you need to decide what's more important: Miss Morelli's *hopes* or this Board's *expectations*. In my opinion Miss Morelli is lucky to have a job at all, Miss Taylor."

"First of all, in all matters related to the school I am addressed by my proper title of Principal Taylor; secondly Nurse Morelli has an employment contract we're obligated to honour; and finally, I would like to hear what the other Board members think."

Before Judith has even sat down conversation erupts as heated opinions are exchanged. With her back straight and her chin up Judith shows she's not in the least bit cowed by Ms. Porter-Wilson. Inside though she's vibrating with anger at how casually this woman makes demands that affect Lila's well-being.

That woman can't contain her frustration at having her meeting devolve into a free-for-all. After having her attempts to silence the discussion shouted down Moira Porter-Wilson flops into her chair with a scowl. Sitting with her arms crossed and her face scrunched up she looks like a petulant brat having a sulk.

Judith is left to marvel at the shocking amount of words a group of women with time on their hands can find to say. Conversations veer off into byroads, anecdotes, something someone once saw on a TV show... it boggles the mind, thinks Judith, trying to contain a smile. She's delighted that none of the comments are concerned with immoral behaviour or compromised standards or any criticism of the School Nurse.

Instead, it soon becomes clear that the winning side of the debate favours being progressive and breaking free of stereotypes. Apparently no one wants to be accused of bias or bigotry, and no one wants to be called old-fashioned or reactionary.

"Besides," one querulous voice opines, "If this Morelli person is a nurse then she's an educated woman who knows how not to get pregnant in the first place, and secondly she'd know how to get rid of an unwanted pregnancy. Obviously having this baby is her choice and with marriage imminent well... what's the problem? More power to her, I say!"

"But the girls–" wails Ms. Porter-Wilson, only to be interrupted by voices claiming *girls nowadays know everything there is to know* and others agreeing *they could teach us a thing or two.*

Pat Johnson stands which quiets most of the chatter. In her loud, cheerful voice she states: "As you all know I recommended Judith Taylor as my successor and I am so proud of the job she's doing. I don't have a vote in this matter but maybe those who do could cast theirs now?"

The Board Secretary jumps at the chance to regain control of the meeting and calls the active members to declare themselves in favour or opposed to Ms. Porter-Wilson's motion that School Nurse, Lila

Morelli, be suspended from her duties. She's barely finished speaking when a resounding cry of *Opposed!* rings out.

While the assembled women are busy exchanging looks of self-congratulation Pat takes Judith by the arm and calls out: "We'll leave the Board to complete its meeting. Great to see you all again! and good night."

Delighted to escape Judith allows herself to be led away and once in the hallway she whispers *thank you! thank you!* to her mentor.

"Oh Judith, of all the nonsense things for Ms. New Broom to complain about... in this day and age!"

"I know, eh? I was wracking my brains trying to figure out who could have committed whatever act Ms. New Broom – I love that, by the way, do you hyphenate it? – considered *moral turpitude.* I even looked up the phrase in the hopes of getting a clue."

"You know, overall I think I'm disappointed and I bet I'm not the only one. I mean, the lure of titillating gossip is always so tantalizing. I'm sure everyone showed up eagerly salivating over the prospect of hearing some dirt."

Laughing, Judith agrees stating: "We are a sorry bunch, aren't we? Look at us, we can't even come up with a decent, I mean indecent, scandal.

I have to admit I was a bit concerned to begin with because Ms. New Broom had everyone hanging on her every word. I thought she'd come into the meeting with allies and was gaining converts."

"Judith something you're going to discover is that volunteers can be among the most censorious people. They figure they're being noble and that that entitles them to take a holier-than-thou attitude.

You'll find that some people will go against their natural inclination just to side with the popular viewpoint, or to go against a personal enemy, and alliances will change all the time.

For example, tonight Jane Branston really came through with that little joke and people joined in on it, but that means Ms. New Broom is probably harbouring a grudge now. At the next Board Meeting something Jane says or does might set her off and force people to take sides.

Committees of volunteers are very difficult to deal with because feelings and sensitive natures are always front-and-centre. I'm afraid Ms. New Broom will be gunning for you."

"Yes, I expect she will although frankly you'd think she'd have the sense to keep her head down after that fiasco."

Pat thinks for a moment then advises that Judith get Samira to dig out the employment contracts. "Just give them a re-read and update as required. You'll need the school's lawyer to okay any revisions and wouldn't I like to be present at the Board Meeting when his bill lands on the agenda? they'll all give Ms. New Broom the stink eye then!"

"Excellent advice as always, ex-Principal Johnson," confirms Judith with a cheeky grin. She can't wait to let Grant know what the tempest in a teacup was all about.

Out loud she says: "Oh and I've got to call Lila, oh no I'll have to wait until the morning. Brian took her to some Businessman's Awards dinner, he's been nominated for an honour. Anyhow I just know she'll laugh herself sick!"

Second Thoughts

Comfortably navigating through the streets of Edgemont Reg explains: "Driving around helps me think." Grant nods, happy to get out of their office and come along for the ride.

He was feeling claustrophobic stuck inside with no leads to work on. They're both getting discouraged as their list of suspects dwindles down.

"When we first started to learn about Gayle Boudreau she seemed like a perfect candidate for murder. I know that sounds terrible but you're a cop, you know what I mean."

"Yeah, I do. Gayle was a thief. She stole drugs from gangsters, she stole cash from her live-in partner, she stole the boyfriends and husbands of women she knew, she stole whatever her coworkers left lying around, she stole her brother's car, and she even stole her kid sister's babysitting money. She didn't care who she stole from.

Gayle earned a decent wage at the club and there's no evidence that she was pouring her cash into drugs, booze, or gambling, so where did her money go? Her chequing account was overdrawn and there's no sign of any type of savings."

Grant thinks a bit then says, "This is just surmise but I think Gayle was the type to fritter her money away on impulse buys or trifles for herself. Like... if she felt like a coffee she wouldn't get a double-double at Tim Hortons, she'd go to Starbucks and pick the priciest offering on the menu."

"Hmm, yeah. Makes sense. Money ran through her fingers like water. What all this means is that Gayle really didn't need to steal, she stole because she wanted to. She got a kick out of it. Like people who lie when there's no earthly reason for it. I guess the label is pathological-something but it sure did set her up to be killed."

"Right? Except we've worked our way through the people she victimized and we're just crossing off one name after the other from our list."

"Then it's someone who never made it to our list in the first place."

"Hmm. There's still the motorcycle gang who, we suspect, owned that brick of cocaine Gayle stole but the timing is really tight between the raid and her death.

We still have that unaccounted time from when Gayle left Eric Littner's apartment until the early morning hours when it looks like she died. A gap that spans anywhere from two to four hours."

"Yeah, I canvassed the area without any luck. There's a coffee shop, a laundromat, a liquor store, and a Mom-and-Pop corner shop but they all shut their doors by 11:00 pm. Every place let me look at their video but I didn't see her walking past any the closed businesses on the surveillance cameras. If she had been there her image would have shown up for sure."

"According to Littner's statement, which he bases on the TV news, she was still in his apartment at that time. Damn, that means she couldn't have gone in that direction."

"Well she couldn't have walked it, that's for sure. She might have gotten a lift part of the way so I drove a few blocks further down and found a twenty-four hour convenience store. It has gas pumps out front so I knew they'd have surveillance inside and out.

I felt hopeful but the place is incredibly busy all the time. The clerks don't remember people unless they cause trouble like a shoplifter, or someone who can't pay, or kids getting high and fighting.

Good Friday night they had a drunk throw up but he was the only memorable person they had. I asked to see their surveillance tapes but they'd already erased Friday night up to midnight. I looked at Saturday until 4:00 am but there was no sign of Gayle inside the store or walking past it."

"Let's drive to that area now. I realize it's hours earlier but who knows? maybe we'll find something that points us in the right direction."

***

After a call to Grant, keeping it short since he's busy with his murder case, Judith phones Lila. To her surprise her friend does not find the *moral turpitude* charge made against her funny at all.

"Okay well, maybe not *funny-haha* but definitely *funny-peculiar*, right? I mean of all the things it could have been I think you being pregnant was the furthest from my mind."

"I hate the thought of these women all gossiping about me–" begins Lila but Judith cuts her off.

"They were all on your side, the vote was overwhelmingly in your favour, Lila. You were supported by someone you volunteer with even before the vote was called, and of course Pat and Eleanor were championing you from the start."

A lengthy silence concerns Judith who continues: "Does this really bother you that much?"

"No-ooo, but maybe I should start my maternity leave early?"

"No, you shouldn't. Or at least you should start when you want to and not be pushed into it."

After making this declaration Judith grabs her purse and slips into shoes and a jacket. She doesn't tell Lila she's on her way but this conversation needs to happen in person.

"Hmmm, I guess..."

"Lila, is there something else bothering you? I don't like to pry but... you're not behaving like your normal self. Listen I'm just getting in the car so I'm going to put the hands-free on, hang on a sec... okay go ahead."

"Oh Judith... my mind is all over the place. I want to marry Brian, really I do and I will but... he's insisting we set a date for the wedding and I'm just not ready to do that. Not yet."

Judith doesn't know how to respond. From the moment the pregnancy test came back positive she expected Lila and Brian would marry as soon as they could arrange it. Being very new to romantic relationships herself she doesn't feel qualified to comment. Once again a silence stretches out uncomfortably.

"Am I wrong to feel this way?"

Hearing the hitch in Lila's voice Judith honestly answers "Lila, I don't know. You know me, I'm hopeless at this kind of stuff. I have no experience to fall back on but... okay let's not worry about whether your feeling is right or wrong, let's try to work out why you're feeling the way you do."

Doubtfully Lila answers, "We can give it a go, I guess."

"I'm going to throw out a few statements and you stop me if, when, I get anything wrong, okay?

Here goes: you're happy about being pregnant... you want to have Brian's baby... you love Brian... you're ready to join the Penner household along with Beth and the new baby... you're ready to get married and be a wife again–"

"Stop. Oh!" Lila sounds as surprised as Judith feels.

"Oh, indeed. Lila do you feel guilty about getting married since Arnie is dead? Ugh, that's pretty blunt, let me rephrase: does it feel too soon to take a new husband or something like that?"

"Maybe that might play a small part... but not really. I mean, it's been over a year and our marriage had already ended.

No, I think my problem is that I feel inadequate or something because my first marriage failed. I believe that's what's holding me back from attempting a second. But we have to get married, I've got a baby on the way."

Arriving at Lila's in record time Judith parks out front and says she's coming in. Hurrying down the walkway to the back of the house she gives a wave to the elderly woman sitting by the front window. Mrs Piernitsky is Lila's delightful landlady, and a good friend to Judith too.

Signalling with her phone to her ear Judith shrugs while the old lady nods in understanding. Stepping round to the back door it opens just as Judith is reaching for the knob.

Lila's watery eyes and pink nose compel Judith to pull her friend into a hug. It's very much *not* Judith's way to voluntarily embrace someone and she feels even more awkward when Lila bursts into tears.

Patting her on the back Judith says: "Lila, Brian isn't marrying you just because you're pregnant. He's crazy in love with you and the baby is a huge bonus. Remember, he's a widower too. He's never gotten this involved with anyone since his own wife passed. I think Brian is the best person to talk this over with. I mean, he knows what you're going through."

Lila pulls away and staring earnestly into Judith's face explains: "Except he doesn't because his marriage was perfect. They were happy, they had a beautiful daughter, they'd built a life together that had everything they wanted. Her death was a devastating blow not a–"

She stops abruptly and Judith tentatively suggests: "A relief?"

"Oh Judith I'm an awful person and Brian will find out. He thinks marrying me will bring him the same happiness he had with Amanda but what if I don't measure up? Did you see how misty-eyed he got reminiscing over her wedding china at our Easter dinner? I'm no saint. What if my marriage failed because of me? What if–"

Judith takes hold of her friends hands and squeezes tight. "I never met Arnie Chalmers, I only have your words to go by, but it always sounded to me like he wasn't willing to put any effort in to your marriage. Did you push him? probably, because you're not the type to stagnate and watch your life waste away. Especially after putting ten year's effort into making it work.

But Lila, I don't think you were the problem, I think it was the drugs he took. I grew up with an alcoholic so believe me, I understand addiction and all the denial and blame and guilt that goes with it."

"But Brian is... he's, he won that award last night. Everyone was happy he got it, you could tell, and I was so proud of him. He's an important person in the community and he'll have expectations..."

Leading Lila back down the stairs Judith seats her on the couch. "Tell me where you and Brian are at in your wedding planning," she demands.

Lila responds to Judith's no-nonsense tone and relates a recent conversation she had with her fiancé.

"I said to Brian *I want to marry you, very very much but it doesn't feel right yet.* I could see he didn't understand and that made two of us. I couldn't explain myself.

Brian was very firm when he said *I want our baby born in wedlock, Lila.* So I told him *the baby will be, we'll definitely get married before the due date.* But then I couldn't find the words to continue. I hated to see the confused and hurt look on his face."

"I can understand that, though. We both know Brian is a straight-forward man so naturally he's frustrated when faced with something that makes no sense to him. He loves you and he's thrilled about having a child with you, of having a life with you. All he knows is that he wants to marry you now."

Freeing her hands Judith takes out her phone and looks up Brian's number. "I'm calling him now," she says but Lila barely responds.

Wrapped up in her misery she simply states: "He's still at work."

When Brian answers Judith gives a concise explanation as to why she's calling and voices concern over Lila's state of mind.

"Let me talk to her," Brian insists so Judith hands her phone to Lila who regards it with apathy. Brian's voice can be heard calling: "Lila? Sweetheart? I'm on my way, honey–" and Lila wails in an outburst of weeping. Judith takes back the phone and tells Brian she'll wait with Lila until he arrives, then she ends the call.

One glance at Lila's state-of-the-art coffee machine *that's a coffee-creator, not a plain old coffee-maker,* shudders Judith. All that shiny chrome with knobs and dials is intimidating enough to dissuade her from attempting to make her friend a hot drink.

Instead she fetches water from the fridge, tut-tutting to herself over the plastic bottle until she twists the cap and realizes it's been re-closed and Lila is re-filling bottles with the filtered water from her tap. She remembers her friend once saying she preferred drinking water out of the bottle to a glass. Judith can't see any tissues so she grabs a couple of sheets from the paper-towel dispenser and decides Lila will just have to make do.

As the crying bout draws to a close both women hear the heavy pounding of Brian's running footsteps. Moments later he's come thundering down the stairs and scoops Lila into his arms then sits on the couch holding her close.

Judith waves away Brian's mouthed *thank you* and heads back to her car.

Mrs. Piernitsky is still at her window, watching the various neighbourhood dramas unfold. She definitely saw Brian Penner race past. The old lady gives a sentimental pat to her chest, over her heart, and nods at Judith who gestures back with a *thumbs-up*. Seeing Brian's anxious concern was reassuring. Judith is confident he'll work it out with Lila.

Down in Lila's basement suite Brian is crooning endearments while he rocks his girl in his arms. With unerring insight he tells Lila: "You aren't betraying Arnie or his memory by marrying me, just as I'm not devaluing my marriage to Mandy just because I've found happiness with you. There will be no comparing because there's no need. What you and I have together is all-new and so, so wonderful, honey."

"Yeah, I know..." she begins but stops herself, looking at him in surprise. "Brian, you're right! I didn't realize why I was dragging my feet but yeah, I think I felt guilty about you, the baby, a wedding... about finding happiness when I couldn't with Arnie. Of not being Mandy..." she huffs out a deep breath that blows her feathery bangs. Meeting Brian's yearning gaze Lila reaches out and the two join in a kiss of reassurance and acceptance.

"Let's set a date." Brian takes out his phone and swipes the calendar app. He wants to pin this down before Lila can change her mind.

***

Reg parks his car in the visitor section at Eric Littner's building and standing out front he and Grant take a good look at their options.

"She might have headed for the road behind this complex. She'd have a better chance picking up a ride there."

"Right, and there's an intersection with traffic lights so I'll find out if there's a camera," says Reg jotting down a reminder in his notepad.

"So you turned to the right and drove that way, right?"

"Yeah right, I turned right. The little strip mall is about two blocks down and the Mac's is another couple of blocks further."

"So, we've got another complex across the road and is that a park on our left? Just past that row of houses?"

"That's a municipal golf course."

"Hmm. Well, let's head that way."

The two men walk to the end of the block and hit the overhead crosswalk lights. Two cars stop but a third flies through screeching its brakes before speeding up again. Reg writes down the licence plate.

Grant knows his partner will follow-up on the violation with Traffic later and he wholeheartedly approves. Failing to stop at a crosswalk is a minor infraction until a pedestrian is struck and injured - or worse.

The golf course is fenced but people have pushed down a section and it's easy enough to get on the grounds.

"There's no one playing," states Grant.

Reg, who is golfer himself, explains the course probably won't open until the May long weekend although the driving range might be open now.

"But the weather's good enough to golf, isn't it?"

"It is, but the grounds – especially the greens – aren't ready to be tramped on. Oh look, there's someone coming our way." The two men stop on the gravel path waiting for a motorized cart to reach them. It's manned by an older man whose red face shows he's in a temper.

"You can't be here!" he hollers while still a good five metres away. Neither detective attempts to answer so the man just yells louder and steering with one hand waves his free arm in a shooing away motion.

Finally arriving and coming to a stop he opens his mouth but both Reg and Grant flip open their police ID wallets before the man gets the chance to utter a word. He deflates but quickly recovers saying: "Good! Are you here about that damage to the fence? I've called the City's insurance department but they haven't sent anyone out yet."

Quirking one eyebrow Grant dryly replies: "We aren't here to fix your fence," and hears Reg turn a surprised laugh into a cough. "But we would like to know how long it's been broken down like that, and if you've had trouble with people coming onto the grounds at night as a result."

"Night and day we have people walking all over the place. Women pushing strollers and when I tell them to get out they jabber away at me in some foreign language. They come here as nannies," he explains, adding: "And I know for a fact they can speak perfect English because I've heard them."

Ignoring this commentary Grant explains: "We're specifically interested in Good Friday night into the early morning hours of Saturday."

"Ah, yes! There *were* some people here then. Criminals, eh?"

"Hmm," Grant murmurs. "That's pretty late at night... were you here then yourself?"

"Not here, but see that black-and-white house over there," the elderly man turns and points to a mock-Tudor two-story. "That's my place. I'm up a few times a night, my age you know, and I did see the flare of a lighter but I couldn't tell you how many were here. It was too dark and those trees block some of the view of this particular area. That's why I never saw who damaged the fence, but that happened during the winter."

"So you saw a light, maybe from a smoker? late at night. Any idea what time?"

The man's face crumples into wrinkles as he scowls in remembrance. In a frustrated tone he admits he doesn't know the actual time. "I've got a digital clock in the bedroom which I'm sure I looked at but the time didn't register in my mind. It wasn't too late though, it was the first time I woke up. Sorry I can't help more," he adds abruptly.

"Oh we're thankful for the information you've given us. The person we're trying to trace is a smoker so you might have added a piece to the puzzle and we certainly appreciate that," Reg assures him.

The old man visibly puffs up. "I came out Saturday morning checking to see if they made a mess but whoever it was didn't throw their cigarette butt down. There was nothing here." Pulling business cards from his wallet he hands one to each of the men before shaking their hands and driving away in his cart.

"You laid it on a bit thick, didn't you?" says Grant with a smile.

"Well, I couldn't do anything less for," Reg glances down at the card and announces: "*Anderson Phillips, Esquire, Shady Lanes Golf Course Senior Member and Volunteer.*"

Grant snorts before continuing: "That light could have come from Gayle. She might have stopped to make her tip-off phone call and smoked while doing it."

"And maybe it wasn't a cigarette. Maybe it was a joint so no butt, or maybe she had a crack pipe."

"Maybe... but we didn't find one."

"We didn't find a phone or a purse either so we have two options: Gayle got rid of everything herself, or some unidentified person took stuff away with them."

"Nobody's said anything about Gayle using crack," Grant adds, doubt evident in his voice.

"Yeah, you're right. Somebody would have said something because the signs are unmistakable and manifest quickly. So, okay, no crack pipe."

The men have headed back and now reach the parking lot. Climbing into the car Grant says: "Let's recap. Gayle left Littner's place fairly soon after 11:00, walking, and phoned the police station at 11:30, probably from the golf course.

That's our surmise since there's no evidence she went in the other direction and someone was at the course late that night so it's plausible.

So where did she go in the roughly forty-five minute span between making the phone call here to getting picked up by Shane Piett on the highway near Edgemont?"

As they pull up to the stoplight Reg directs Grant's attention upwards saying: "Look, there *is* a traffic camera here. Let's get on to the division asap to see if that camera can answer our question."

***

Judith, like Reg, finds driving around is conducive to deep thoughts and soul-searching. Her circumstances, and lack of funds, meant she missed out on the teenage rite of passage of getting a drivers' licence. It wasn't until she'd finished college and was earning a paycheque that she took driving lessons.

She passed the test on her first tary and bought a little car. That was a milestone event. It represented so many things, but mostly the joy and freedom she felt sitting behind the wheel, just her car and the open road.

Speed isn't an issue for Judith. She doesn't need to go fast to feel free but she does like an uncluttered road. The Old Banff Coach Road is a favourite route – no congestion and easy-going speed limits – so long as driving conditions are good. It's easy to access from Edgemont and the familiar trip allows her to let her mind wander.

She starts by thinking about how Lila's been stalling on setting a wedding date because of her worries. Her foolish unfounded worries that Brian might find her lacking.

Those thoughts lead to Judith acknowledging her own reluctance to schedule her wedding and trying to understand why.

What she told Grant is true, she doesn't want to take anything away from Lila and Brian's big day, but there's more to it than that.

She realizes she's acting scared. Not of marriage to Grant, she's fully confident in the strength of their love, but of the actual wedding. Of the planning and the arrangements, the timing, the guest list, invitations, choosing a venue, colour schemes, flowers, a cake, a meal, wedding party attendants, a photographer, a reception with music and dancing, and she's so far over her head, it's terrifying. Utterly overwhelming.

Grant's been pushing her for a date. He claims his sisters are nagging him but Judith isn't convinced. She knows Grant enjoys organizing things. Judith does as well but the things she likes to arrange are spreadsheets and columns of figures, not people who need entertaining. *And that's okay*, she decides. *I don't have to pretend any of that interests me. Maybe it should, but I was never the little girl who played make-belief bride games.*

Breathing deeply she tells herself *I can admit that I don't want to study wedding-dress catalogues, read bridal magazines, or pin pictures to some digital bulletin board. If Grant and his sisters are willing to take it all on well, why not let them?*

Coming to that decision feels as liberating as having this open road all to herself.

While Judith is out driving her cares away Grant and Reg are eagerly pursuing the traffic camera lead.

The Last Witness

The traffic camera shows Gayle standing outside a bus shelter. The route has finished for the night so the Detectives figure she's hoping to hitch a ride.

While stopped at a red light an older woman, driving alone in a compact car, keeps looking over at Gayle. When the light turns green she pulls up to the curb and opening the passenger window is obviously speaking to Gayle. Asking for directions? no, Gayle gets in the car so the woman must have offered her a lift.

Traffic division has a clear shot of the licence plate and after some strong-arming over complaints about it being Friday afternoon Reg gets the name and address of the female car owner. Luckily for him the woman has a landline because the reverse directory doesn't include cellphone numbers.

Abruptly standing Grant says: "Don't call, Reg, let's just go there. We'll meet the woman face-to-face. After all, she's a witness and maybe an important one."

They practically repeat their previous trip since the witness lives in the same area, but on the other side of the golf course. Pulling into the shared driveway of a duplex Reg remarks that *the lady* was *almost home and maybe she brought Gayle with her?*

Grant doesn't bother speculating, he's eager to hear what their witness, Ms. Anita Whitelaw, has to tell them. Reg has to hurry to catch up with Grant who has already climbed the steps and rung the bell.

They hear a female voice talking and a moment later the door opens a couple of inches. They see a woman holding a black Persian cat and telling them to make sure her other cat doesn't get out. Both men look down to see – and hear – a Siamese attempting to escape around its owner's foot.

"We're with the police–" begins Grant with his ID in hand but the woman, presumably Ms. Whitelaw, interrupts him to say *hurry inside and mind the cat.*

"When I saw that there were two of you I assumed you were... well, I suppose you still could be, but not here for that purpose, not proselytizing?" she rambles.

"Er no, we would like to ask you some questions. You are Ms. Anita Whitelaw?"

"I am. Questions? Oh my! I know I haven't done anything wrong so this will be interesting. Please come in to my little front room and oh! you aren't bothered by cats, are you?"

Murmuring *no, not at all* they follow her into the first room on the left. The bay window is covered with lacy sheers that allow a good view of the street while affording the occupant some privacy. A calico cat is stretched out along the window-ledge, catching the last of the sunshine.

A well-worn Queen Anne style of armchair sits in the alcove along with a small table. The shelves underneath hold library books and a boxed puzzle. There's a folded newspaper on the chair and a bag of knitting on the floor. The effect is a cozy, lived-in ambience.

An elderly cat has taken possession of that chair and the woman fondly pats its head bragging: "The minute I get up he's claiming the warm spot!"

Leaving ownership to the tom she seats herself on a spindly chair while gesturing to the love-seat. It's a tight fit for the two big men but the room is too small for a full-size sofa. Having already spotted four cats and wondering if there are more they haven't seen yet Grant is momentarily distracted by the thought of Judith turning into a *cat lady*. He decides, with relief, that she's really not the type and nods to Reg to begin.

"Ms. Whitelaw we're here to ask you about a passenger you gave a ride to on Friday, Good Friday, night at–" he stops suddenly when the woman loudly exclaims *Oh her! I might have guessed.*

Patiently wearing an enquiring look Reg waits for her explanation.

"Yes, I did give that... that woman a lift. I saw her waiting for the bus but transit stops at 11:00 pm although sometimes on holidays it runs later but that's in the summer, not on Good Friday, so I thought to myself *she's going to have a long wait.*

I opened the window and asked if she needed a ride somewhere. She jumped at the chance, marching right over and getting into my car. Naturally I was curious about her. I figured she couldn't have lived in the area or she'd know about the busses. But I didn't like to pry so I just introduced myself hoping she would explain."

Ms. Whitelaw pauses to reflect that *she never did say why she was there waiting at that stop.*

"Where did she ask to go?"

"Oh to Edgemont. She didn't ask me to drive her all the way there, she just said that's where she was headed and I said I didn't mind making the trip.

I explained that I have plenty of time and I wouldn't feel right leaving a young lady stranded on the road late at night so I would see she got home safely. That seemed to amuse her... she was really a very peculiar girl.

Once she was in the car and close enough for me to get a good look at well... she wasn't really a girl any more, closer to thirty I'd guess, and she wasn't at all like anyone I've ever met."

"So you introduced yourself and she said..."

"That her name was Gayle." The two men exchange a satisfied glance that their hunch had panned out.

"Now we noticed you were almost home when you gave this Gayle a lift."

"That's right but I was, oh it's hard to explain. Normally when I'm out I'm always happy when it's time to come home. I get anxious about the cats on their own, you see, but that night I just... I felt restless, and driving Gayle home seemed like the right thing to do. My *good deed for the day* except *no good deed goes unpunished* as the saying goes."

The black cat is still in her owner's arms being stroked while the Siamese continues to meow at the closed front door. Neither the calico nor the old orange cat are paying any attention to the humans.

Reg needs to use all his skill to elicit a coherent accounting from Ms. Whitelaw. Grant is reminded of the two teenagers, Tasha and Shane. Like them Ms. Whitelaw digresses, following every conversational by-road and often ends up losing her train of thought. Finally the story emerges and it's a shabby sort of tale.

Ms. Whitelaw had been at Bingo (not to gamble, of course, but to support the Church) and afterwards she joined a few other players who went for a drink.

"A *nightcap*, we called it, and I was enjoying myself but they were three couples and after awhile I started to feel a bit like a fifth-wheel so I said my goodnights and was heading home when I saw that Gayle woman waiting for a bus that wasn't coming."

In her convoluted way the older woman explains how she spoke to Gayle of the loneliness that comes with age when you're on your own.

"Married to my job, I'm afraid. I wasn't keen on taking early retirement but they explained about needing to move up the younger people or else they'd leave, and the severance package was, well... very handsome. So I'm quite comfortable, but sometimes time hangs heavy on my hands, another well-used expression."

Grant forces himself to sit quietly but he's finding it a challenge. He successfully resists the urge to demand *get to the point, woman!* and coughs to hide a smile as he pictures Anita Whitelaw's face if he did bellow at her.

"So I said that *I try to be cheerful because you never know, I could meet Mr. Right tomorrow at a gas station or the grocery store or even the library,*" she peers up at Reg who gives her an understanding nod.

"Well, that Gayle was just downright rude, laughing at me. She said, and I don't think I'll every forget her words, she said *the gas station or grocery store? what a small world you live in. You won't ever meet anybody. You're too boring, too timid, too dull, and too old.*

Officers I have to admit I'm a bit ashamed of what I did next. I know it was wrong of me but all I could think was *I'll show you timid* and I yanked the wheel to drive onto the shoulder and I told Gayle to get out of my car. She had the nerve to argue! insisting *you said you'd drive me to Edgemont--* and, well, I completely lost my temper and started yelling. Screaming, I'm afraid. I ended up shrieking at her to *get out! get out! get out!*"

Ms. Whitelaw sighs deeply and an unattractive blush stains her cheek. She isn't wearing any make-up and the colour flames against her pale skin.

"I know what I did was wrong. I left her stranded – the exact opposite of what I wanted to do – but this woman was just so awful."

"I don't blame you at all," states Grant speaking up. Ms. Whitelaw turns her gaze to him and seems to notice for the first time how handsome he is.

Smoothing her hair back off her forehead her expression turns cautiously hopeful as she answers: "Oh! You don't think it was terrible of me?"

"No, not at all. You were very kindly going out of your way and she insulted you. Needlessly insulted you, and in your own car, too. Sheer nastiness and bad manners. What happened next?"

Feeling vindicated by Grant's remarks despite his abrupt way of speaking Anita Whitelaw perks right up. "Well, she got out and made a rude gesture with her hand," lowering her voice she whispers, "*with her finger* - you know what I mean - and then started walking west on the side of the highway.

And can you credit this? she left the car door wide open! I had a struggle, finally having to undo my seat-belt in order to reach far enough across to grab hold of the handle to close it."

Now it's Reg's turn to emit a fake cough to cover up his chuckle as he thinks *that Gayle!* Ms. Whitelaw explained that she then made a u-turn to head back to Calgary.

"I know that's not allowed on the divided highway, those paths are for emergency vehicles only, but there was no one around, not even those great big trucks. I just didn't feel like I could pass her."

"Perfectly understandable, Ms. Whitelaw. Could you give us an idea of the time at this point?"

"Certainly. I have a clock in the car and I looked at it to calculate what time I'd be home. I dropped that ungrateful woman off at five to twelve and I know the cats must have been worried. They have a very good sense of time you know, and I'm never out that late at night. It must have been about 11:35 or :40 when I picked her up."

"Well that's been very helpful," Reg says rising to his feet with some difficulty from the soft couch.

"Oh really? It was?" Ms. Whitelaw asks, brightening again.

"Tremendously," states Grant in a tone that puts an end to the conversation.

Of course they need to spend another ten minutes while the woman fusses about not having offered refreshments, belatedly offering them now, asking if she needs to sign a statement, but finally they make their way to the door and almost escape when Ms. Whitelaw suddenly asks:

"How did you know about me?"

Reg explains about the camera at the traffic light and tracing her licence plate. Ms. Whitelaw spends so long considering this that he wonders if she's going to complain about violating her privacy. Instead the woman beams at him with a lovely smile and congratulates them both for *being awfully clever.*

With another round of *thank you and goodbye* the detectives squeeze through the door, just managing to keep the frantic Siamese inside.

"So that piece of the puzzle is filled in, Grant. Shane Piett picked up Gayle at midnight give or take a minute. She left him at the theatre which is walking distance to where her body was found. I wonder why she went to the school at all, though? She was almost home."

"Except it wasn't her home any more, was it? And I can't imagine what was going through her mind. I mean, she'd just blown off a woman for being too old and minutes later she finds herself facing the same kind of prejudice from some teenager."

"I think that's what they mean by karma."

***

Judith is quick to answer when she sees Lila's name come up on her phone. She's been anxious about her friend but didn't like to intrude, especially with Brian there. The moment she hears Lila's voice she knows everything is going to be all right.

"Judith! Saturday, June 5th. That's my wedding day. It's less than two months away and we need to get dresses. You know you're my maid-of-honour, right? Brian says we can get married at a restaurant, isn't that crazy? but convenient, we don't have to go to City Hall, in fact we can't go to City Hall. I'll explain it all later but right now I have to call my parents so Mom can book their flights.

I've got to let Mrs. Piertnitsky know, too. Did I tell you she's invited Mom and Dad to stay with her while they're here? Isn't she just the best? Okay I gotta go now, but let's go shopping tomorrow. Phone me in the morning."

Lila has barely drawn a breath while saying all that and Judith gives up trying to get a word in edgewise. Before she realizes it the call is disconnected. Bemused, she sees her phone shows the recent incoming call lasted for 30.18 seconds.

She wants to call Grant, but knows he's out chasing down a lead. She'll give him the good news when he gets home tonight. For now she scrolls to the Calendar app on her phone and checking the dates decides Saturday, September 4th sounds good for their wedding date.

Oh, but it's the Labour Day weekend and that might be inconvenient for guests, she thinks. *Unless we get married on the Friday instead? I'll talk it over with Grant's sisters.*

Wedding Planners

Judith calls Lila first thing to say they'll have to go shopping tomorrow because she's already invited Grant's two sisters to come over to her apartment for coffee. She doesn't mention the reason, that she's told them it's to discuss her wedding, just that they've both agreed to come so she can't back out of the invitation now.

"Oh. You might have said something yesterday, Judith."

"I would have but I couldn't get a word in edgewise before you hung up. You didn't even give me chance to say congratulations!"

Lila giggles admitting: "You're right, sorry! Tomorrow is okay for shopping. Today Brian and I can go check out the restaurants on our short list. I know you'll want to get ready for your company but let me just tell you one thing: my parents are over the moon. Mom's already called back to give me their flight times and they're so excited."

"I'll bet they are. And it's great your Mrs P is putting them up so you can visit with them each day until the wedding without having to drive or even get dressed up to go out."

"I know. She really is the best landlady ever."

"And she'll really miss you too, Lila."

"Yeah she will. But I'm so glad I got her new tenants all squared away."

"What do you mean? Who?"

Lila gasps saying: "Didn't I tell you? Omigod I can't believe—are you sure I didn't say—?"

"LILA!" Judith hollers, exasperated.

"Okay, okay this is brilliant: Eddie and Tanya are moving in."

"Our teachers? Oh that *is* good news. I know they got engaged—"

"And they want to be together but he shares a place with two other guys and she still lives with her parents. The cost of a nice apartment for the two of them in Calgary is astronomical plus paying for parking and they would have the commute, whereas here they can live in a detached house for about half the cost. You know they're both paying off student loans, still.

Mrs. Piertnitsky's family is thrilled to hear a young man will be on the premises as protection and to help out with any little chores. Although I'm quite sure Tanya can just as easily shovel the walk in winter and mow the grass in summer. Plus take the garbage and recycle bins in and out, that sort of thing."

"Oh it does sound like a perfect solution. They'll have a comfortable home, close to work, and will be fed well, too!"

"Yeah it really is ideal. They haven't set a wedding date but even once they do marry I think they'll still stay on at Mrs. P's while they save for a downpayment."

"Nowadays a lot of young people don't plan on being homeowners. Or at least not the single family, white picket fence version."

"I have to say I'm glad Brian has good handyman skills because there's always something that needs doing when you've got a house.

Anyhow, I'll let you go. Phone me later when you're free and we'll set up a time for tomorrow. I'm trying to decide on Chinook Centre or Cross Iron Mills for dress shopping. Maybe we'll have time to do both? Bye!"

Judith can't help but smile at her friend's enthusiasm. Lila is definitely back to her old self and it's wonderful.

Judith is surprised that she isn't experiencing butterflies over this visit from Grant's sisters considering what she's planning to say to them. They're nice women who she's met in person twice now, and she and Grant have had many Zoom calls with his family, especially over the holidays.

She likes the twins, Adelaide called Addy and Abigail called Abby, very much, but sometimes feels intimidated. Probably because of the way they communicate with each other. She doesn't know if they're on a special twin wavelength or if it's simply a sibling thing. She has no experience with that.

The two are only six years older than her which Judith knows because the women are planning a big joint celebration for their fortieth birthdays.

Judith brings out a tray of coffee to add to the plates of cookies, sliced cake, and fresh fruit laid out on the coffee table in her living-room. Plates, forks and spoons, and napkins, are all stacked to the side so her guests can help themselves.

Judith warned Grant to stay away while the women visit. *You're welcome to come say hello once we're finished with our business but I don't want you poking your nose in until then,* she said being firm.

Grant tried to point out that it's his wedding too, but Judith dismissed that comment saying *everyone calls it the Bride's Day so good try but no, the three of us are perfectly capable of managing without you.*

Judith relates this conversation to her soon-to-be in-laws who remark that *not only would Grant have hogged the conversation but he'd also eat way more than his share of these scrumptious desserts.*

"Oh I already fixed him a plate and put it in the fridge. He was in a snit when I chased him out so before you leave I'll call him to come back and we can bring him up-to-date on what's happening."

The women have their younger brother's fair colouring although their blonde hair is more yellow than his. Studying both faces Judith explains she finds it fascinating to see the strong family resemblance the three of them share.

"Yet what's masculine in Grant's features is feminine in yours. It's especially amazing to see this physical connection when you're an only child like me."

"George mentioned both your parents have passed away but are there no grandparents, aunts, cousins, no one?"

"Addy stop calling him George, you know he doesn't like it," corrects her sister.

"That's what I've called him his whole life–"

"And ever since his teens which were what? about twenty years ago? he's asked to be called Grant. So why don't you call him that?"

"Because it's silly, Grant is our surname."

"Not any more," points out Judith. Her input has a comical effect on the sisters with Addy pouting and Abby grinning.

"She's right. So think of it that way and call him Grant. Write *Grant* on his birthday cards."

"And what do I put on the envelope, hmm?"

"Just put *Grant*. The postie goes by the address not the name or salutation."

"Growing up did you two find yourself falling into roles that defined you as the older sister and you as the younger sister?" Judith asks.

Two identical pairs of eyes turn to her with quizzical expressions. "I'm being nosy, I know, but I'm curious. The way you're talking right now it's easy to figure out who is the eldest but are you always this way?"

Abby giggles saying: "She's got you there, Addy. Judith, you are 100 percent right. Addy always takes on the bossy *I'm older so I know best* role."

"Hmph, well you sure like being the spoiled baby when really you're just lazy."

"Okay, stop! Forget I said anything," Judith placates them holding up her hands with one palm facing each woman. "I don't want to get in between you two because I need your help."

Immediately the sisters end their bickering to give her their full attention.

"What's up, Judith?" asks Addy at the same time Abby says "How can we help?"

"It's about this wedding we've got coming up."

"Oh yes, we've got some ideas to run past you–"

"Addy! let her talk."

Addy looks contrite and pressing her lips tightly together gestures for Judith to continue. Judith can't help but smile at the antics of the two sisters.

"You're going to need more than some ideas because I have none. I truly am alone in this world with no relatives at all. I do have my very good friend Lila, but she's getting married herself and will be having a baby right after. I can't ask her to help when she's going to have her own hands full.

See, the thing is I've never planned any kind of celebration or party. Well, I rarely attend them and I've never actually been to a wedding. All I know is from what I've seen on TV or read in books. Now, let me start by saying I'm not religious but am perfectly happy to have a church wedding – any church – since that's what Grant wants."

"Does he? Which church?"

"He's never actually said but... he acts like that's his expectation so I guess I just assumed."

"Hmm, our family really isn't much for religious stuff, none of us are churchgoers so... I take it Grant, there see Abby? I *can* call him Grant. When I remember, that is. Anyhow, Grant doesn't want a Registry Office wedding, he wants a religious ceremony, right?" At Judith's nod Addy continues: "Maybe we could select a venue and get a non-denominational minister?"

"Maybe we could even do it outdoors?"

"That sounds great!" enthuses Judith. "See this is what I mean, you guys know about stuff like this and really... well, I was wondering if instead of buying us wedding presents would you consider planning the wedding for us and making that your gift? From the two of you?"

Judith knows she's made the right choice when the women's eyes light up at the prospect.

"Oh this will be so much fun!"

"We'll choose a colour scheme and make all the selections for flowers, clothing, invitations, menu... but we'll come to you for confirmation first."

"No, that won't be necessary. We've met a few times now so you've got an idea of what I like and how my taste runs, and of course you know Grant better than I do! I mean look around this place – it isn't the latest fashion or brightest colours, and look at me – I'm not a frilly girly-girl. So I want you to go ahead and arrange it all. I defer to your expertise!

My maid-of-honour, although she'll be a matron-of-honour by then, will be Lila Morelli. She'll have just had her baby so maybe a dress that's loose and floating so she doesn't have to diet like crazy to fit it? Oh! I just realized I don't know who Grant will ask to be his best man. You'll have to ask him about that."

"We'll meet with Lila, I better take her phone number now," says Addy unlocking her phone.

"Right, we'll have to schedule the bridal shower with her too," puts in Abby.

Judith frowns but, thinking of Grant, decides not to complain about that.

"I don't have anyone one else for attendants but I was thinking, between the two of you there are nine kids so how about if they make up the rest of the wedding party? That way they all get to play a part, no one is left out."

"Oh that's brilliant, right Addy?"

"It's not an even number though, five boys and four girls... Wait! we don't have to divide them into sides, they can all come down the aisle together and just stand in a row behind Grant and Judith."

"Oh yes, I can see that. They'll be all dressed up and so pleased with themselves. Oh they'll look so cute!"

"And they're pretty much old enough to know how to behave, at least for an hour or so."

"Well of course my children are perfect but we can work on yours..."

The women happily laugh at the joke and Judith notices that all her tension and most of her nerves about the wedding have disappeared. She's content to sit back and listen while the sisters talk over each other to plan, argue, insult, brainstorm some ideas, finally agree and then all is well again.

So many details, thinks Judith mentally patting herself on the back for offloading the chore. She pauses in her self-congratulations when she realizes the sisters don't see it as a chore at all. *The two of them are born party-planners. Maybe it runs in the family?* she muses. *They're making lists and loving every minute of it.*

"If we do have an outdoor wedding there will need to be a canopy or something... some sort of canvasc shelter for protection in case it rains..."

"Oh and nowadays it's almost impossible to serve a meal with so many people being faddy over their diets–"

"There's nothing faddy about Celiac disease, Addy!"

"Oh you know I didn't mean that, that's serious. I meant vegetarian, vegan, lactose-intolerant, Kosher, Halal, gluten-free, nut allergy, low sodium, low carb, Paleo, ketogenic, the list just goes on and on."

Judith doesn't realize she's spoken out loud until both women howl with laughter when she says: "Too bad we can't just ask them to pack their own lunch."

"What about no meal at all?"

"Don't be ridiculous, people expect to be fed!"

"No, people expect an open bar so their drinks are free."

"No drinking," states Judith.

Addy and Abby both gasp, their faces wearing identical looks of horror as their forks clatter to their plates.

"Sorry! didn't mean to say that," Judith exclaims, her cheeks burning in shame. "It was an automatic reaction. Of course people can drink and we'll provide the drink, of course. Of course. Grant enjoys a drink. So do Lila and Brian. I don't... well, I've never tried but no, I never will. But that's just me..." her voice trails off.

Addy says: "You know what? Where is it written that every wedding means guests have to dress up, go the Church, hang around while photos are taken, go eat a big meal while listening to speeches, drink toasts, dance, cut a cake, throw a bouquet, I think those are all the usual elements, right? but we don't have to do all of that or even most of it.

We could have a beautiful outdoor ceremony, photos and cut the cake, eat it, drink champagne for toasts, and then send everyone home."

"No party?"

"No, the whole point is the actual marriage, the vows ceremony, there doesn't have to be a party."

"Won't that look cheap?"

"Oh! Well, we could insist absolutely no gifts, no cash—"

Judith tells the sisters what Harry said. "We were given a very good suggestion about that. A young man told us we could ask our guests to make a charitable donation in lieu of gifts."

"That's a wonderful idea!" the twins exclaim.

"Actually, we could amass quite a big donation—" states Addy with Abby adding: "Plus the money that would have been spent on the reception, too. It will be a sizeable amount going to a good cause."

"Yes! Because you know, I really don't need an eight place-setting set of china, do I?" confirms Judith.

Both sisters nod in agreement although they have no idea where that comment came from.

"What about Grant? Will he like a cocktail party idea?"

"Ah, Grant."

"Yeah, baby bro is a bit of a traditionalist, isn't he?"

"You're right. He definitely will expect us to feed everybody. Well, we'll just have to get open-minded caterers who won't complain when customers make their demands. Now, about the cake. I've got some ideas about that."

"Judith what date have you two chosen?"

"We haven't pinned it down yet but I was looking at the calendar and thought September 4th but it's the long weekend so maybe the week before or after? or even on a Friday? What do you think?"

While the sisters discuss the ramifications of various dates Judith gets a very pleasant picture in her mind of Grant standing at the altar wearing a tuxedo.

Resolution

"You're looking chipper today, good news?" asks Reg.

Nodding Grant replies: "Two things. One, it looks like I'll be getting married late August or early September, and two, I think I know what happened when Gayle Boudreau died."

"Okaaaay," Reg draws out the word. "First off, congrats on kind of setting the date. Well to having it narrowed down to two months, anyhow." Grant flips him off. "That's an eight- or nine-month engagement which seems pretty normal. What was the hold up?"

"Judith. She wants Lila and Brian to have their big day first, and then we'll announce our date and everyone will have to hustle."

Reg tilts his head with a speculative look on his face before a huge grin takes over. "You've got yourself a good girl, Grant. She's a keeper."

Grinning himself Grant happily nods in agreement.

"So where are you going on your honeymoon?"

"We've pretty much decided on a European cruise. There are quite a few options so we'll search things out on the Internet–"

"A cruise? Are they safe since Covid is still lingering? Hmm, my advice is go talk to a travel agent. Find out the facts and if it sounds okay then get a bunch of brochures, you'll enjoy going through them together.

Everything on the Internet looks wonderful but an agent can give first-hand reviews and recommendations."

"Oh you're right. Thanks Reg, that's a good idea. You know, I'd forgotten about the problems the cruise ships had with quarantines and all that. We might need to postpone the two-week honeymoon until a later date.

Hmm, we could still take a long weekend at one of the Hot Springs in BC."

"You've got a lot coming up in the near future: house-hunting, a wedding, honeymoon, moving... and a crime to solve before you go."

"Ah, about that. That's the other thing that's put a smile on my face. It's partly something Judith said that led me the conclusion I've drawn about Gayle Boudreau.

You won't know this, but Lila was dragging her feet about setting a date with Brian. Both of them were married before, both widowed, but whereas Lila was on the verge of divorcing her husband Brian and his wife were very happy together until she got sick. Brian's wife died of cancer many years ago. Turns out Lila was worried that she wouldn't measure up to his memory of married life."

"But surely she knows that Brian won't be making comparisons. I've met the man and he's a straightforward kind of guy. If he's told Lila he loves her, which I have to assume he has since they're getting married and have a baby on the way, then he means it."

"That's right, and Lila knows it too. She was just overcome by the negative thoughts in her head. Bleak thoughts of despair that weighed her down. I thought *maybe it's hormonal because of the pregnancy?* because both of my sisters were, every single time. Haywire emotions and crazy thoughts.

Then I remembered that Gayle was also pregnant and maybe irrational with it as well."

"Hmm, completely different scenario but go on."

"That's when Judith said to me *Grant, think about it. Try to imagine what thoughts were in Gayle's head. Everything was going against her which must have felt pretty oppressive... and depressing. She had the means and the motive to end her life so do you really think this is a murder case?*

And that's when I realized of course it isn't murder."

"Grant, the victim's mood might indicate that suicide is likely but her emotions aren't facts."

"True, but let's recap what Gayle *believed* the facts to be." Holding up his fist he pops out his thumb saying: "One - she knew when she phoned in the drug tip that she'd burnt her bridges at work.

Two - her mother told us that was the longest she'd ever held a job so quitting would have stirred up some feelings.

Three - then she finds out that her married lover is willing to pay up just to keep his wife from getting hurt. Turns out he really is in love with her. He doesn't care about Gayle getting hurt.

Four - after Gayle fought with her mother she didn't have anywhere to stay so she shows up at her recent boyfriend's place, expecting she can convince him to take her back, but he's turned stone cold towards her. She even begged for a second chance.

He said he told he *had* loved her but she killed that feeling. How would she feel hearing that? Especially if she's already emotional and behaving erratically?"

His hand is wide open, fingers splayed as he concludes: "Five – she's pregnant, she's on her own, she's been told she's old, she's feeling down and doesn't see much of a future for herself."

Reg is nodding along at each point and now says: "You think... you think she gave in to despair and overdosed on purpose?"

"From what we've learned about her personality I think she had a sort of a *Russian Roulette* attitude to taking the drug. If she died, well the phony suicide note was planted in her locker and that would *muddy the waters*, so to speak. If she survived, she'd take that as a sign not to give up."

"So what does that make it? accident or suicide? Was it a cry for help that went fatally wrong?"

"No, I think it was more like a *to hell with you* statement. I think that even feeling as miserable as I suspect she must have been – maybe even because she was so unhappy – she wanted to set things up to cause as much trouble as possible.

On the day she died she made a point of seeing and arguing with all of our suspects. I don't think it was deliberate, but who knows what thoughts went through her mind when she ended up all alone? Then it might have felt providential that she'd managed to put everyone in the frame.

She called in that tip and I think she ditched her phone afterwards. So my conclusion is that Gayle was looking at herself coming up on thirty with no friends, and no husband or kids. She'd sabotaged her career, broken family ties, and maybe she was having second thoughts about terminating the pregnancy?"

"Grant, I think you're right. All of that gibes, it makes sense. But listen, instead of outlining the reasons why it could be suicide how about we flip that idea around and figure out why it couldn't have been murder?"

Grant leans forward, interested, and gestures for Reg to continue.

"First of all there were no marks on the body indicating that Gayle was held down and that the drug was forced into her mouth. No bruises around her lips or jaw.

Secondly, all of the suspect's motives have fallen apart. The married lover's wife already knew about the pregnancy and the live-in boyfriend certainly has the means to replace what was stolen. Plus he doesn't strike me as the type to take risks.

If there was something going on between Gayle and her mother's boyfriend Norm it didn't break those two up. Her brother and sister could have sneaked out of the trailer to meet up with Gayle behind the school but when did they plan this rendezvous? and how likely is it that overprotective Harry would take Didi out in the wee hours?

While the club was being raided by the Drugs Squad Gayle's time is accounted for up until shortly after midnight. Assuming the cocaine belonged to the club owners then it's possible they would kill a thief to *send a message* - but how would they know where to find her? They'd want to make sure everyone knew it was murder, and she'd probably have been badly beaten first.

The girls at the strip club aren't going to kill a co-worker for pilfering trifles, and even if Sol Stein had some motive that we never discovered he didn't have the opportunity.

So overall... hmm. Overall I agree that the only conclusion is death by a self-administered drug overdose."

"Yes, you've covered every argument for and against each verdict, Reg."

"It's always sad to see a young life lost, and dammit thirty is still young, but the fact that there really was no murder is good news. Well, *lesser of two evils* sounds better."

"I'm perfectly happy to let a verdict of death by misadventure, an accidental overdose, stand. And, sorry to say it, but Harry and especially Didi are now free from Gayle's malign influence and the trouble she brought – and would continue to bring – into their lives."

Weighing everything Grant said Reg tips his head in acknowledgement.

"I think Judith pointed you in the right direction because yeah, you've solved this, boss. It's not exactly an Easter blessing, but..."

"But spring is an uplifting time, and our ex-suspects can hope for new beginnings and fresh starts."

***

It's Saturday now, thinks Gayle as she walks down the sidewalk of the silent village. The light from a TV shines in one solitary window in the apartment block on her left. To her right is the forest. *Dark and creepy*, in her opinion.

Saturday of a long weekend, Easter weekend, and I've got no where to go. I have no home and nobody wants me. Gayle's steps slow as she contemplates her immediate future. It looks pretty bleak.

She figures she might as well keep walking until she gets to the Trailer Park. If worse comes to worse she can curl up in one of the lawn chairs. Realizing it's too cold to do that Gayle shakes her head at the idea. I'll just *knock on Didi's window till she wakes up and lets me in.*

Satisfied with this plan Gayle picks up her pace. She knows the Edgemont School for Girls is on the other side of these woods. The Trailer Park is within walking distance because Didi goes to school here and makes the trip back and forth every day. In fact, there's a cycling path that shortens some of the distance.

Catching sight of the old sandstone building Gayle is impressed by its size and how neatly the grounds are kept up. Lilac bushes are blooming now and Gayle loves their smell. She seems to remember the yellow of forsythia as well but only the various shades of purple and mauve from the lilacs are showing now. And there's a bush of white lilacs too. The smell is overpowering and sweet.

I wish I'd gone to a school like this. Maybe I'd have hung on longer, had better teachers and got better grades. My school was no good. Didi's lucky.

Gayle crosses the road and walks onto the front lawn of the school. She follows the aromatic bushes all around the side of the building to the back. Her feet are killing her in her high-heeled boots so she plops herself down on the steps to have a rest before finishing her journey.

I guess I can't go back to work tonight although... maybe I can? After all, they can't pin that tip to the cops on me, I didn't give my name. I don't even know if the bar got raided. Maybe they didn't bother. If they didn't, I can just give that brick back to Solly. He won't stay mad at me, he never does.

I don't like my job much any more but it pays pretty good. And I sure don't like the women I work with but some of them got steady boyfriends who were once customers. That's how Cindy got Clay and he married her. I've always got plenty of guys coming on to me, wanting to date me, so maybe I should seriously think about settling down. Since I'm so old, according to that stupid kid tonight.

Yeah, I'll just show up for my shift like nothing's happened because probably nothing has. Huh, if Solly wants to get rid of me he'll have to fire me. Then I'll get severance pay. And he'll pay because he won't want any complaints to the Labour Board.

You gotta be confident to get by in this world and take chances. Nobody's going to stick up for me, nobody ever has. What's the worse that can happen?

Gayle props her elbows on the step behind so she's laying supine with her long legs crossed at the ankle. She only has a couple of cigarettes left and smokes them one after the other, just letting her mind drift.

When she stubs out the last butt she fishes around in her pocket in case another fell out of the pack but no, the only thing she finds are the two pills she was given.

They're supposed to be like Ecstasy-on-Crack, she recalls somebody saying. What the hell, I'll take 'em both and be super high and super happy, she reasons as she knocks them back.

For Gayle Boudreau the Easter long weekend of 2021 has already ended as she falls into a state of euphoria so relaxing her body forgets to breathe.

Epilogue

On July 23rd Robert Elijah Penner arrives a week early with minimal fuss and weighing an even 8 lbs.

Bethany is delighted to finally have a baby brother; the proud parents have already fallen deeply in love with their son; and his *bisnonna [great-grandmother]* happily calls him *Roberto* despite his grandmother saying: "No, no Mama, his name is Bobby."

From the Author

I hope you enjoyed reading *"Evildoing at Easter in Edgemont"* and will share your review to help other readers discover it.

Thank you so much! I really appreciate it.

I'd love to know your thoughts! please email me at: AuthorDellaNorth@gmail.com

Don't miss out!

Visit the website below and you can sign up to receive emails whenever Della North publishes a new book. There's no charge and no obligation.

https://books2read.com/r/B-A-RNHX-NNHJG

BOOKS 2 READ

Connecting independent readers to independent writers.

Also by Della North

Village of Edgemont
A Deadly December in Edgemont
A Fatal February in Edgemont
A Sinister Spring in Edgemont
A Crimeless Christmas in Edgemont
Evildoing at Easter in Edgemont

Standalone
Village of Edgemont Cozy Mysteries

Watch for more at dellanorth.ca.

About the Author

Della enjoys mysteries that won't keep her up at night, have a hint of romance, and a satisfactory ending. Preferably in a series.

She and her partner live with a tuxedo cat in the sunniest city in Canada, nestled in the foothills of the Rocky Mountains.

Books in this series:
1 "**A Deadly December in Edgemont**"
2 "**A Fatal February in Edgemont**"
3 "**A Sinister Spring in Edgemont**"
3.5 "**A Crimeless Christmas in Edgemont**"
4 "**Evildoing at Easter in Edgemont**"
Available in eBook, Paperback, or Audio.

Also *bundled-to-save* in the "**Village of Edgemont Cozy Mysteries Books 1-3**" collection.

Read more at dellanorth.ca.

www.ingramcontent.com/pod-product-compliance
Lightning Source LLC
Chambersburg PA
CBHW020952180626
46814CB00003B/1047